His eyes, often narrowed, appeared never to miss a detail. *Appeared.* Because the truth was, Clouseau often saw little that was of importance; so distracted was he in an attempt to maintain his dignity while fulfilling whatever his current case might be that he had a tendency toward . . . what is the French word? *Klutziness.*

He had not yet met the man whom he would consider his great ally—an ally destined to become an adversary—but Jacques Clouseau nonetheless shared the central flaw of Chief Inspector Charles Dreyfus: maintaining a dignified image was of key importance in the lives of both men.

There remained, however, a vital difference between these two public servants. Charles Dreyfus would make any sacrifice to maintain his dignity, but Jacques Clouseau would sacrifice the dignity that was so important to him if it meant solving a crime—if justice could be served.

During a career distinguished by a surprising number of cases that had reached successful conclusions, Jacques Clouseau had acquired detractors who unkindly insisted that within his hard head resided a decidedly substandard brain. Even his supporters would not argue with that assertion, though they would often point out that—within a chest swollen with perhaps too much pride—beat a great heart.

THE PINK PANTHER™

A NOVELIZATION BY MAX ALLAN COLLINS
BASED ON THE SCREENPLAY BY LEN BLUM AND STEVE MARTIN
AND THE STORY BY LEN BLUM AND MICHAEL SALTZMAN

HarperEntertainment
An Imprint of HarperCollinsPublishers

The text of this book is consistent with the film script available at the time of printing. Please be aware, however, that some of the film scenes may have changed in post-production.

HARPERENTERTAINMENT
An Imprint of HarperCollins*Publishers*
10 East 53rd Street
New York, New York 10022-5299

ISBN: 0-06-079723-1

First HarperEntertainment paperback printing: July 2005

Printed in the United States of America

Visit HarperEntertainment on the World Wide Web at
www.harpercollins.com

10 9 8 7 6 5 4 3 2 1

Respectfully dedicated to
Blake Edwards—
father of
Peter Gunn,
Professor Fate,
and
Jacques Clouseau

"Comedy is a man in trouble."

JOSEPH LEVITCH

THE PINK PANTHER™

ONE

Fatal Flaw

On the day that would lead to the greatest mistake of his notable career, Chief Inspector Charles Dreyfus of the Police Nationale of France basked in a sunshine both literal and figurative.

He did not follow football—soccer, like all sports, held no interest for him—nor was his life consumed with any passion other than what he considered a selfless dedication to his chosen profession . . . and what his detractors had determined was a lust for self-glorification.

In any case, his attendance at the semi-final game of the international championships had nothing to do with whether France defeated China to advance to the final game. Nor did it reflect national pride, such as that exhibited by the normally distinguished individual beside whom Dreyfus sat—Clochard, the Minister of Justice; or for that matter, the President himself, seated beside Clochard.

Both dignitaries were—like all the fans in the Grand Stadium—anticipating the start of the competition and cheering like schoolgirls at the "big game." Behind the placid mask of his coolly handsome face, Dreyfus concealed a mild contempt for such lack of self-control.

And yet these men mattered to Dreyfus, and explained his presence in the VIP box, amid darkly anonymous Secret Service agents. That the chief inspector was here, in such august company, indicated an honor in the offing, specifically his recent nomination for the national Medal of Honor.

Dreyfus had been so nominated seven times.

Circumstance and politics had conspired against him, however, and he had not yet prevailed; still, none of his countrymen could boast of such a feat—seven nominations! That itself was an honor—wasn't it?

Wasn't it?

But for a man of dignity—and dignity was so very important to Chief Inspector Dreyfus—it pained him to notice the relative shabbiness of his suit compared to that of the Justice Minister.

This, however, was mildly galling. It did not

compare to the spike of irritation Dreyfus experienced upon the entry into the vast arena of Yves Gluant, the coach of the French team. The narcissistic and (by Dreyfus's way of thinking) conventionally handsome boor carried himself like a movie star—and the crowd responded with an ovation as excessive as it had become customary.

What had this man ever accomplished, Dreyfus wondered, to deserve such love and respect from his fellow citizens? Chief Inspector Dreyfus had personally put away scores of dangerous criminals, and supervised hundreds of arrests that had resulted in convictions. Dreyfus had led his men into battle against Mafiosi and Yakuza and even these new Russian criminals—whereas Gluant would today take his soldiers onto a field against the Chinese . . . to kick around a little white ball.

As the stadium announcer introduced him, Gluant stepped from his team's box to greet the crowd, granting them a smile and a raised fist. Sunlight caught the jewel on the ring of his upthrust hand, as he conspicuously turned toward each section of the crowd, which went wild in successive waves.

Most of the crowd, that is: Chief Inspector Dreyfus remained seated, arms folded, forcing a tiny smile, in case anyone was looking. Mustn't appear bitter.

Bitterness was, after all, the mark of the small minded. And Dreyfus was big. So very big.

As the popular coach turned to face each side of the madly cheering stadium—giving everyone present the opportunity to take in the diamond on his ring, the storied jewel seemed to wink at each attendee personally. Dreyfus could only inwardly shake his head, thinking of how sad it was that the great nation of France had descended to the worship of acquisition. Let the Americans follow such shallow pursuits if they liked! But for the French to view a stone, a diamond, as somehow the symbol of its success on the field of sport . . .

As absurd a concept as it was distasteful.

And yet even Dreyfus—if he could be honest with himself (which he of course could not)—would have had to admit that this jewel was indeed special. This was the most famous stone in all of Europe, perhaps the world, with a history so fabled, so bloody, as to put the Maltese Falcon to shame. From the Middle East to Asia, from America to France itself, the celebrated diamond had cut a swath of death, betrayal and destruction.

The irony was that the stone's size and perfection did not constitute its most famous aspect; in fact, the diamond was not "perfect" at all—at its center, a tiny flaw could be perceived, which some ancient Arab potentate had said resembled a leaping panther.

A pink panther.

Dreyfus watched with detachment and yet with the eye for detail of an exemplary detective. Throughout the entire stadium, he alone noticed that the team lined up on the field included one player who flashed the tiniest tellingly negative expression as their coach joined them.

This was Bizu, perhaps the most muscular of the players on the French team—effective but reckless, a quality characteristically reflected by his trademark untamed shock of black hair. His eyes were fixed on the coach, but to the average observer, Bizu merely cast upon his leader the intensity of gaze normal in a true competitor.

Yet Dreyfus saw—sensed—something else.

Bitterness.

Envy.

These were emotions the chief inspector could easily recognize . . . in others.

Dreyfus watched with well-concealed contempt as the arrogant Gluant strode toward a box seat in the front row where—surrounded by fans (and security)—sat a stunningly beautiful young woman in a glittering outfit more appropriate for a rock video than a sporting event.

This, then, was Xania, world-famous diva of pop, the beauty of her milk-chocolate skin matched by the dark chocolate of her expressive eyes and her exquisitely coiffed mane. At this moment, many considered her the most desirable woman on the planet.

Right now she was signing an autograph for a child, allowed in to provide a photo op, of which the press corps took full advantage. With Gluant heading toward Xania, the crowd's attention was set upon the two members of what the tabloids of Europe and America alike had crowned the current celebrity couple of choice. Even the Chinese contingency—the most imposing figure of these dignitaries, Dr. Pang himself, the solemn and distinguished head of the Chinese sports delegation—gave their full attention to the paparazzi's favorite lovers.

And who could blame this crowd of sports fans? After all, sport was conflict, and the conflict on the minds of many right now involved this idyllic romance of beautiful people that had recently degenerated into what America's *National Inquisitor* had termed XANIA AND GLUANT'S LOVE AFFAIR, adding ominously STORMY WEATHER AHEAD?

Even Dreyfus found himself caught up in this moment, and when Xania stood in her front-row seat to turn coldly toward the superstar coach, he surprised her by taking her hand, pulling her to him, and kissing her passionately.

The crowd erupted into cheers that had nothing to do with soccer.

Even Chief Inspector Dreyfus smiled—he was, after all, a Frenchman . . .

. . . but also a detective, and instinctively he switched his gaze toward team member Bizu, whose name had also been linked in the tabloid press to the pop star. Even at this distance, Dreyfus could sense, could *see,* the jealousy, Bizu's eyes flashing in the sunlight like the Pink Panther itself.

Dreyfus could not see—had no reason to seek out—the coldly staring eyes of a gaunt, narrow-faced individual who appeared to be nothing more than a well-dressed businessman: Raymond Larocque. This "businessman," however, was attended by a large, rather ominous Asian bodyguard, whose presence was the only indication that Larocque might one day find himself on the radar of Chief Inspector Charles Dreyfus.

But that day was not today, an afternoon consumed with a football game so exciting even the detached Dreyfus found himself watching with something approaching interest. By the end of the regulation time, Dreyfus was actually sitting forward on his seat—the score tied, the game going into those extra minutes so vividly described as "sudden death."

The Justice Minister leaned toward Dreyfus between plays and said, "Are you enjoying yourself, Chief Inspector?"

Dreyfus summoned an enthusiastic smile. "For a true fan like myself? It is almost too much."

Then a Chinese player took a shot, which looked to be dead certain . . . but a goaltender for the French made a spectacular save, sending thousands of fans to their feet, the Justice Minister and the President included. Dreyfus, however, missed this moment, remaining seated, caught up in the task of brushing lint from his lapel.

At this tense moment, from the sidelines, Gluant could be seen waving his hands, signaling a player substitution.

His decision—to take out the great Bizu, and replace him with the unseasoned young forward, the boyish blond Jacquard—was not popular. Disappointment traveled across the crowd in murmuring ripples.

But this was nothing compared to Bizu's reaction.

The wild-eyed, wild-haired star pushed past the boyish blond forward and made a bee-line for Gluant, getting in his coach's face, screaming until his own face grew scarlet and the veins and cords in his neck stood out in sharp bas-relief.

Gluant remained comparatively calm, and seemed cooly in control as he made a reply to his furious player that only sent Bizu into a further fit of fury, the star throwing a punch.

The coach slipped the thrust, but returned it, and then the two were at each other, players and referees and security people swarming the pair, trying to pull them apart.

The trainer and assistant coach managed to pry Bizu's hands from his coach's neck; the two team staffers were holding back the beast Bizu had become—eyes wild with rage, teeth white and flashing in a face gone purple now, hair like black snakes writhing—as the handsome, unflappable Gluant merely gestured for the game to continue.

And when the game came to its climax, Gluant was proven right about the young forward named Jacquard.

The ref blew his whistle, a Chinese player threw in the ball, only to have a French player intercept, kicking the ball upfield in a long, high arc as the young forward made a mad dash toward the Chinese goal, in a race seemingly against the laws of physics themselves.

On their feet, too astonished even to cheer, the crowd gasped as Jacquard leapt high, realizing just in time that the round sphere was coming down not in front but behind him . . .

. . . and turned a somersault in midair!

With his face staring at the ground coming up at him in dizzying speed, he nonetheless kicked the ball into the net with the back of his heel.

A split second of amazed silence was followed by a roar of pleasure, as the French fans screamed in ecstasy, shaking fists at the heavens, whether in pleasure or defiance, who could say?

Around Dreyfus, the Justice Minister, the President, even the Secret Service were on their feet, cheering, a few doing distasteful American "high fives."

The Justice Minister glanced down at the seated chief inspector and said, "Can you *believe* it, Charles?"

"No," Dreyfus said, summoning another smile. "It is a miracle."

Grinning ear to ear, the Justice Minister returned his attention to the field, applauding madly.

And Dreyfus checked his wristwatch.

On the sidelines, chaos ruled.

Jacquard, flush with victory, sped to where Gluant embraced him. Coaches, players, photographers and the more demented, determined fans swarmed upon the new star player and his star-making coach, driving them back to the sidelines where in the front row a somewhat startled, even taken-aback Xania recoiled from the throng.

The police were doing their best, but when the celebrated coach needed them most, their crowd-control duties were not enough . . .

Dreyfus, eyes sharp, finally stood, even as the others in the VIP box had settled back into their seats.

He had seen Gluant stiffen, straightening up,

the coach's face—even at this distance—taking on a chilling blankness that resonated within this skilled investigator's being.

And Chief Inspector Dreyfus, with a new and terrible enthusiasm, ran from the box, down flights of stairs and—gathering security as he went—led a small army onto the field where he, like those crowd-controlling police, was much too late.

The coach of the winning team had fallen to the grass.

All around people scrambled, and in the stands of fans the screams gathered into something resembling the earlier cheering, but not the same, not at all the same, something sad and even sinister having entered in, as if a nation were crying out in collective anguish.

Dreyfus bent over the corpse of the handsome coach—for indeed a corpse this was, a small dart sticking from the dead man's neck.

The presence of this object was matched in significance by the absence of another.

Dreyfus's eyes made the journey down a lifeless arm that seemed to be pointing, though that hand may have singled out any one of thousands. And it was not the forefinger that mattered, was it?

It was the finger with the white band of flesh where a ring had so recently been.

The team's trainer was suddenly at the chief in-

THE PINK PANTHER

spector's side. "My God, someone's killed him! Someone has murdered Gluant!"

"I'm afraid it's more serious than that," Dreyfus said, rising. "Someone has taken the Pink Panther."

TWO

The Case of the Missing Hot Dogs

Again the sun shone bright on this lovely Parisian day, the magnificent white marble of the Palais de la Justice gleaming and winking, like the Pink Panther itself.

In the spacious, richly furnished office of the chief inspector of the Police Nationale, huge blow-ups were propped on easels, photographic representations of the body of Coach Gluant, in particular the wound with the dart, as well as various angles on the crime scene and assorted shots of the people in attendance. Other images showcased the fabulous missing stone itself, in shots of Gluant's hand as he greeted the crowd, as well as file photos of the fabled gem that had become, in the eyes of many, a symbol of France's victorious football team . . . a symbol now gone— with its heroic coach.

Unlike the fallen coach, however, the symbol was still out there, "alive" in a sense, and recoverable . . .

Spread across the chief inspector's desk was evidence, *not* of a crime, but of the feeding frenzy of both the local and the world press. Newspaper headlines screamed: FOOTBALL GENIUS MURDERED; GLUANT SLAIN FOR DIAMOND RING; and PINK PANTHER STOLEN BY KILLER. In many of these same papers, in particular the European ones, a smaller front-page headline told of another, seemingly unrelated story: GAS-MASK BANDITS WREAK HAVOC IN ITALY.

"At least," Chief Inspector Dreyfus said, "those thieves are staying in Italy, well out of my jurisdiction—another problem of that magnitude, I *surely* don't need."

Dreyfus, resplendent in formal wear, stood with arms out in crucifixion mode, giving himself over to a tailor making the last fitting of the tuxedo the chief inspector would wear to the imminently upcoming Medal of Honor ceremony.

Nearby, patient as a priest, stood Dreyfus's loyal deputy chief, Renard. Shorter than his leader, the bespectacled Renard attended his master, poised and ready. The deputy was highly valued by Dreyfus . . . not just for his efficiency, but for his lack of ambition; Renard had made quietly but eminently clear that the pressures his superior officer bore were nothing he envied.

"I know it's the single most important thing in your life," Renard said gently.

Dreyfus's eyes rolled skyward, as if God Himself had made a hobby out of vexing him. "Three weeks away, the ceremony! Three weeks!"

Gesturing to the surrounding blow-up photos, Renard said, "I did not mean the medal, sir—I meant the Gluant case."

Dreyfus, still at the tailor's mercy, glanced sharply at his deputy. "Is there a difference? This case, tied to our nation's fanatic interest in football, could *easily* drag me down!"

Renard patted the air, lending his usual calming influence. "No. No, you will get it this time. You deserve it."

"Don't patronize me! This is a first-class disaster. What are my options, Renard?"

A tiny shrug. "You have two options, of course."

"Which are?"

Renard's eyebrows lifted; he held out his hands, open-palmed, as if literally weighing the possibilities. "Pass the case on to a subordinate, or take it on yourself. There is no greater detective in France, after all, than Charles Dreyfus."

This obvious flattery Dreyfus chose not to characterize as patronizing, preferring to accept it at face value. "But, Renard—both of those options are rife with risk."

The deputy shrugged. "If you catch the killer, the medal is undoubtedly yours."

"And if I *don't* catch the killer?"

Renard said nothing, but flinched a smile.

"Exactly! If I officially take on the Gluant case, but do *not* find the killer before the ceremony, I will be an ass, the object of ridicule, an embarrassment to the government . . . and the medal will undoubtedly go to someone else."

"Again," Renard said quietly.

"Again! . . . And if I *do* assign the case to someone else, and *he* finds the killer . . ."

Another tiny shrug. "The man who finds Gluant's killer will be a national hero."

"Yes, Renard—and he will undoubtedly receive the medal that is rightfully mine!" Dreyfus stepped away from the tailor. "It's a nightmare—you understand, I seek not glory for myself, but for France?"

"Of course, sir."

He turned to the framed portrait of Charles de Gaulle, visible between two crime scene blow-ups.

"What would the general do . . . ?" Dreyfus thought for several long moments. Then his eyes widened and flashed, his nostrils flared, and a faintly demented smile spread. "My God . . . there is a *third* option."

"A third option, sir?"

Dreyfus's smile was proud of itself. "What if I assigned an *idiot* to the Gluant murder?"

Renard, his eyes slightly magnified by his glasses, blinked. Twice. "An idiot, sir? Intentionally? And why would this—"

"Because an incompetent fool . . . an unimaginative, by-the-book, low-level incompetent would just plod along, the media following his every step . . . watching him get *nowhere!*"

"I see," Renard said, not seeing at all.

Dreyfus began to pace, unaware that his pinned-together tuxedo was shedding pieces, the tailor following behind with concern, but too intimidated by the chief inspector to speak.

Legs bare now, Dreyfus struck a pose that he imagined to be dignified and impressive. "It's *genius*, Renard! . . . While this boob is treading water and splashing it all over the media, *I* will secretly put together a task force of the finest investigators in France—led by myself, personally!"

"Ah," Renard said, beginning to smile in understanding.

"We will work around the clock, hunting down the killer . . . but strictly sub rosa. We will undoubtedly find the killer in time to secure the medal for . . . for the rightful recipient."

Renard's head cocked slightly, an eyebrow arched. "And if you don't?"

"*That* is the genius of it! The boob I've assigned will take the criticism! I will make vague statements about my disappointment in this individual, who had come highly recommended to me, and so on . . . and indicate that I will take over personally . . . but at such a late date that the medal will not be forfeit."

"It *is* clever, sir."

Like the Pink Panther, the chief inspector had a flaw at his center: a desire for recognition that outstripped his numerous finer qualities. So it was that Charles Dreyfus, in his attempt to make himself look good, made a bad mistake.

His greatest mistake . . .

"And I think I know just the man, the perfect boob for this job . . . Before I rose to this office of distinction, I heard bizarre tales of an officer who wrought such havoc that he was banished to the hinterlands. He has for some years bounced from one province to another, one small village to another . . . generating some of the most amazing reports of incompetence the Police Nationale has ever known."

Renard's confusion was obvious. "How ever has he managed to stay on the force?"

"Ah, Renard, you know as well as I do, we live and breathe in a civil-service world—tenure alone protects him. And on occasion, rare occasion, he has produced results. The countryside is littered with those who despise him, with a small minority who are deluded by his manner, which I am told projects a level of confidence seen only in the highly skilled . . . or the utterly foolish."

Renard's half-smile indicated he had joined the conspiracy. "I see—but this quality of confidence will aid in making him a presentable public choice for the case."

"Yes. A man of the people—a fresh face."

"Where can I find him, sir?"

"I'm not sure which poor French citizens are burdened with his presence, currently—check the computer. Find him. Bring him to Paris!"

"What is his name, sir?"

Jacques Clouseau, Gendarme Third Class, rode through the cobblestone streets of the modest village of Fromage in the passenger seat of a paddy wagon.

Looking like a figure stepped out of another time, Clouseau—in his spotless dark blue gendarme uniform with white cap, brass buttons ashine—projected a quiet dignity. The premature white of his hair was not shared by the dark dapper mustache which added to an air of competence that its wearer prized. Of average height and build, Clouseau nonetheless projected a larger-than-life presence; and many a member of the fairer sex had found him handsome.

And yet, there was something a little . . . wrong. The confidence of his smile seemed somehow counterfeit; the shrewd cock of a lifted eyebrow might on closer examination look mildly skew.

His eyes, often narrowed, appeared never to miss a detail. *Appeared.* Because the truth was, Clouseau often saw little that was of importance; so distracted was he in an attempt to maintain his dignity while fulfilling whatever his current case might be, that he had a tendency toward . . . what is the French word? Klutziness.

He had not yet met the man whom he would consider his great ally—an ally destined to become an adversary—but Jacques Clouseau nonetheless shared the central flaw of Chief Inspector Charles Dreyfus: maintaining a dignified image was of key importance in the lives of both men.

There remained, however, a vital difference between these two public servants. Charles Dreyfus would make any sacrifice to maintain his dignity; but Jacques Clouseau would sacrifice the dignity that was so important to him if it meant solving a crime—if justice could be served.

During a career distinguished by a surprising number of cases that had reached successful conclusions, Jacques Clouseau had acquired detractors who unkindly insisted that within his hard head resided a decidedly substandard brain. Even his supporters would not argue with that assertion, though they would often point out that—within a chest swollen with perhaps too much pride—beat a great heart.

This is not to say there were not casualties in the path of this inadvertently great detective. Even now, after having deftly removed the portable flashing light from the glove box, Clouseau placed it on the roof of the paddy wagon, oblivious to the need to fasten it in place. Thus the light, though flashing bright red, did not serve sufficient warning to the old lady knocked off her feet by it.

Clouseau was too focused to take in such peripheral inconsequentialities. He had a case to solve. A robbery.

Ah, a mystery! How the chase of the hunt energized him! It energized him almost as much as the hunt of the chase . . .

"Faster, Andre!" Clouseau demanded. "Faster—crime waits on no man! So justice, she must not lag!"

Through the streets they sped, rounding corners on two wheels. Finally the paddy wagon pulled into the modest town square, pulling up tight to a curb that hugged the nearby wall. This minor detail the great detective did not note, so of course he slammed his door into the brick—making only a small dent.

"Swine wall," he muttered. Then to his driver he said, "Are you an idiot? There is a wall here! Pull up."

The young driver followed Clouseau's command.

"That is much better," Clouseau said. "Andre, I do not mean to be a harsh mistress. But, my young friend, when you have walked the streets of crime, as have I these many years, you will learn that no detail is too small."

With that Clouseau opened the door and walked into a parking stanchion, so common on French streets, but an apparent mystery to the great detective, whose testicles rang like sore bells.

Still not seeing who his assailant was, Clouseau chopped the air with expert karate blows, taking a step back. Noting the stanchion— "Swine stanchion!"—he turned to Andre, on the sidewalk behind him now, to inquire, "What fool placed this public menace here?"

"The police department, I believe," Andre said softly.

"Take a note . . . Not a mental note! Take out your pad, man!"

Andre obeyed.

"Remind me to write the memo advising the Police Nationale to distribute leaflets describing this public nuisance. Some fool could be injured."

"A possibility," Andre admitted.

Clouseau recovered quickly from such mishaps—a combination of his intense training in the martial arts, and the large areas of his body that had gone numb from frequent injury.

Skillfully avoiding the next stanchion—"They are clever, these stanchions, Andre!"—he approached the scene of the crime. His heart beat with excitement. A case! A new case!

As he moved along the picturesque street, where the tourists seemed to outnumber the townspeople, Clouseau carried with him a riding crop, with which he beat a gentle rhythm against his thigh.

Andre, who had been working with Clouseau only a short time, inquired, "Are you a horseman, sir?"

Confused, Clouseau said, "Of course not! I am a policeman. Do I look like a horseman?"

"Well, you *are* carrying a rider's crop . . ."

Clouseau paused and put a kindly hand on the younger officer's shoulder. "You will learn, Andre, as you walk these streets of mean, that a policeman must be respected. *This*, she is a symbol of power!"

He raised the crop swiftly, and unknowingly slapped a tourist in the face. The man cried out, and the woman at his side went to his aid, gazing at the two passing gendarmes with amazement and, perhaps, horror.

"You see, Andre?" Clouseau smiled. "Power."

He did not sense the angry tourist striding up behind him, and his next gesture of the crop whapped the tourist in the stomach, doubling him over. When the man cried out, the two gendarmes wheeled, Clouseau's instinctive karate chops slicing the air.

Then Clouseau straightened, his mustache twitching as he smiled. He gestured to the tourist, who appeared to be bowing to them. "You see, Andre? Respect . . ."

Moving into a small courtyard, with Andre behind him, Clouseau's keen eyes took in the scene . . . and the suspects. A hot dog vendor stood under an umbrella; nearby were patrons, couples mostly, seated at small checker-clothed tables, enjoying the beautiful weather in this beautiful country. A central well—perfect for lovers to cast in coins, and make a wish—provided a romantic touch that Clouseau could well appreciate.

A pair of gendarmes who walked this beat were waiting to assist the investigator from headquarters.

Clouseau approached the agitated vendor, a mustached heavyset fellow in an apron. A slender younger man, apparently the vendor's helper, stood behind the wagon.

"I am Clouseau," the great detective said to the vendor. "I am told you have a case for me."

"I am missing a case."

Clouseau frowned. "But has there not been a crime?"

"Yes! I am missing a case. Of hot dogs."

Eyes narrowing, Clouseau said, "Ah, I see. It is

the missing-case ploy. And how many hot dogs are missing?"

"They come two dozen to a case."

"And how many does this make?"

The vendor blinked. "Twenty-four?"

"Twenty-four! Yes. And why do they come twenty-four to a case?"

The vendor shrugged. "I . . . I don't really know!"

Clouseau slapped his thigh with the crop—a bit too hard. "Ow! Yes! This is the correct answer."

"It . . . is?"

Clouseau raised a gently lecturing forefinger. "You see, had you known . . . you would be a suspect."

The vendor's assistant offered, "Each case has two packages. Each package has a dozen hot dogs."

Slapping his thigh again, Clouseau said, "Ow! . . . *You* are a suspect! . . . Andre, take him to the van . . . Perhaps a trip to the headquarters will make you more forthcoming."

Too confused to be angry, the vendor's helper walked off in Andre's custody.

Clouseau said to the vendor, "You are clearly a man of intelligence. This is your business. It is your business to know your business."

The vendor shrugged. "Well, yes. It *is* my business."

"Yes! Precisely! Ow." Clouseau moved closer to the man, almost conspiratorial in manner. "How do you analyze the situation, my friend?"

"Well . . . someone's stealing my hot dogs."

From nearby, a local gendarme said, "A clear violation of statute 209A."

Clouseau warily eyed the source of this interruption. In a voice that was perhaps louder than need be, he said, "Statute 209, part A: a restaurant serving raw meat must be licensed for such; a brasserie serving cheese must also purchase an equal volume of ice; no café can have tables less than three feet from the boulevard. Section B and C are unimportant . . . they were repealed in 1897."

The vendor was taking all of this in, astounded by the depth of the officer's knowledge.

But still Clouseau went masterfully on: "Section D, however, remains in force—all streets bordering an abattoir shall be outfitted with a blood gutter terminating in a municipal sewer or licensed drainage ditch!"

Then the detective whirled to the gendarme who had dared interrupt him and said, "So I can only assume that you meant to invoke statute 212C."

The gendarme squinted. "How does that statute read, sir?"

Clouseau thrust a pointing finger skyward. "Unlawful to steal hot dogs!"

The gendarme hung his head in shame.

"Do not despair my young friend. One day you, too, may have the steel trap mind of Clouseau . . . Now, my dear vendor, tell me something about this . . . this 'business' of yours. This—what is the technical term? This hot dog business."

"Well," the vendor said, "someone comes up to me and says, 'I would like a hot dog.' "

"I see . . . I see." Clouseau moved in, eyes wide. "And then?"

"Uh . . . then I sell them a hot dog."

Clouseau nodded, thinking, thinking, thinking. "I believe I have the grasp of the situation . . . may I summarize? You sell someone the hot dog."

"Yes."

"And then they . . . ask for the hot dog? This does not make sense to me."

"No, first they ask, then I sell it to them."

"Yes, yes. Clever. You are a clever man of business, monsieur. My congratulations . . . And so, into your well-ordered life, into this business so brilliantly conceived, comes the crime! The one who does not ask . . . who does not buy . . . *the perpetrator!*"

"But . . . *who*, Officer?"

Clouseau put his arm around the vendor's shoulder. "My little friend, if I may call you 'my little friend'?"

"Of course."

"Crime . . . she is lurking. Somewhere. Perhaps

there! Perhaps . . . here. I will need to question your patrons."

"But, Officer . . . they are Americans. A tour came through for lunch. I speak very little of the English."

Clouseau backed away, chuckling. "Oh, ye of petite faith! Am I not Jacques Clouseau—master of language? I speak eight languages . . . and one of them, as it happens, my little friend . . . is the English." And to make his point, he said, "I am, in fact, fluid in the English."

The vendor said, "Don't you mean 'fluent'?"

"Not at all. Listen to the English flow from my lips . . ." And Clouseau spun toward the crowd, seated at their little tables, and said, in English, "Everyone! Up against zuh well!"

As Clouseau glanced at the vendor, pleased with himself, the patrons shared glances and shrugs, and got to their feet and moved quickly to the well, and stood with their backs to it as best they could.

To the nearest gendarme, Clouseau said in French, "What are they doing?" To the suspects who had formed a ring around the well, he demanded in English, "What are you fools *do*-ing?"

The vendor said, "You told them, 'Up against the well.'"

"I said 'Zuh well! Zuh well!'"

And he thrust his riding crop toward the nearest wall.

"Ah!" the vendor said. He turned to the suspects and said, "The wall! The wall!"

Soon the suspects had gathered against the brick, facing Clouseau.

"*Back* to zuh well!" Clouseau demanded.

A tourist nearby squinted and said, "You want us to go back to the well . . . ?"

"No, no, no! Hands to the . . . brick. Now! Do not an-gare me. It is not a pleasant thing to see, the an-gare."

"Anchor?"

Grimacing, Clouseau gestured with the rider's crop, making a circle, and finally they got it.

Under his breath, Clouseau said, "Swine suspects," and began to pat them down.

He was on the first suspect when Andre returned from the paddy wagon.

"Ah! My young assistant . . . watch and learn. You must not be shy, you know? You must be thorough . . . What's this?"

Clouseau, patting down the man with whom he'd recently conversed, had worked his way up the legs to the crotch.

"Swine . . . In the van! . . . Andre, move quickly. Take him to the van."

The tourist was saying, "Ah come on! What's the idea? What are you, some kinda French pervert?"

"That is 'prefect.' And I am but a lowly pubic servant. Though I do hope to advance. Take him! Take him!"

The next suspect—possibly the companion of the previous suspect, a male—was a female. A comely one, at that. But this did not dissuade the great detective from his duty. And though he searched thoroughly the same area used by her possible accomplice for smuggling purposes, he found nothing.

"You madame, are free to go."

Within fifteen minutes, the search was complete—it seemed a dozen couples were involved in the hot dog smuggling operation, although none of the women had any incriminating evidence on their persons.

Thus it was that Clouseau stood with Andre at the rear of the crowded paddy wagon, in which the vendor's assistant had been joined by twelve American males—one of them a clever devil, a transvestite—all squeezed in, like hot dogs in a package. They left behind a dozen women, utterly astonished by the level of Clouseau's police work.

Andre said, "I don't understand, sir . . ."

"Ah, but you will, my young friend! When we take these suspects to headquarters, and give them a strip search . . . one of us will have the big surprise. Perhaps even . . . a dozen of the big surprise!"

"Yes, sir," Andre said.

But at headquarters, the biggest surprise awaited Clouseau, and it was not in the pants of any of his suspects: it was a call from Paris.

THE PINK PANTHER

He was wanted.

Jacques Clouseau was wanted, to work on a case so important to France herself that it would make the Case of the Missing Hot Dogs seem utterly ridiculous.

THREE

Enter Inspector Clouseau

When the townspeople of Fromage gathered to
bid adieu to Jacques Clouseau, brandishing placards of fond farewell, there were few dry eyes
among them. There were, however, numerous
neck braces and leg casts.

Upon bestowing assorted hugs and kisses, and
after delivering a final speech of advice for Andre
(his latest pupil), Clouseau—spiffily attired in his
dark blue gendarme uniform and white-trimmed
cap—climbed into his tiny Renault and headed
for the big city, the big time, the big case . . .

He was spared the sight of many of those same
townspeople hurling aside their placards to re-
joice in an orgy of applause and jumping up and

down, including those in leg casts. And yet some genuine fondness lingered.

Even Andre had to admit that Clouseau had, after all, cracked the Missing Hot Dogs Case. The very first suspect, the vendor's assistant, had admitted the theft . . . though the twelve other suspects were highly offended by the strip search. Or anyway, eleven of them were—the transvestite seemed oddly complimented.

As for Clouseau, like many a rural traveler, he began hunkered over a map, even as he drove. Soon he found himself lost on a country road; but he persevered and, before long, he was indeed in the city, heading for the famed Arc de Triomphe, passing by the Seine, then staring wide-eyed with wonder as he drove around the Traffic Circle, finally getting a good close look at the famous Eiffel Tower.

What separated Clouseau from the average rural traveler, however, was that within an hour, he again found himself lost on a country road.

But a helpful rural gas station attendant managed to point Clouseau back in the direction from whence he'd come, and at last, the great detective re-detected the city of Paris.

In particular, he detected the Palais de la Justice.

Despite a life spent fighting crime, Clouseau was at heart a naive schoolboy, and he drank in this magnificent sight, this monument to his proud profession; his entire life had led up to this moment. It was as if the city, and this grand building, welcomed him with open, giving arms, symbolized by the generous parking space seemingly waiting just for him, right out in front.

Clouseau, however, was not one to spit in the face of generosity. He took his time parking, displaying a skill no city dweller might have expected from a simple country sort. True, he did tap the car ahead and behind—poorly constructed vehicles, whose bumpers fell off, requiring Clouseau to emerge from the smart little Renault to kick them from his path ("Swine bumpers!"). And he was not exactly sure how he managed, at one point, to find himself completely sideways in the wide spot. Nor had he meant to wind up backward in it, either.

But when he was done, he had parked, and proudly.

And he managed to smile, despite the annoying car alarms that had gone off in those faulty vehicles fore-and-aft. That was one thing he did not look forward to, being transferred to a metropolitan beat: this terrible noise pollution. He would write a memo, suggesting something be done.

Soon, ramrod straight, a proud example of the French police officer, Clouseau entered the outer office of Chief Inspector Charles Dreyfus. The chair behind the reception desk, however, was empty. Casting his ever-observant gaze around the spacious waiting area, Clouseau quickly spied a lovely young woman . . .

. . . standing on the desk.

Perched at a somewhat precarious angle, she was attempting to hang a large gilt-framed portrait of her distinguished superior on the side wall.

Clouseau took the liberty of approaching the desk and the young woman, planting himself beside a well-turned calf, his cap respectfully figleafed before him. Purely as a matter of maintaining his trained detective's skills, he catalogued the woman's attributes.

Her blue blouse with jacket and short skirt were both stylish and business-like, and managed to do justice to her slenderly curvaceous frame. Brunette with a short 'do, delicately pretty in a gamine-like way, she wore glasses that gave her a studious cast, emphasized by the concentration she lent her task.

Speaking directly to her lovely legs, Clouseau said, "Good morning, mademoiselle. I see you are engaged in a project of the interior decoration."

"I'll be right with you," she said without looking at him. "Sorry . . . The Minister of Justice sent around a new picture of himself, the other day . . ."

Indeed an elaborately framed portrait of the dignitary—whose image Clouseau had seen frequently in the press—rode the wall nearby.

"But it was larger than the chief inspector's,"

she continued, her application of the framed portrait to the wall exhibiting excellent muscular control in Clouseau's opinion, "so Chief Inspector Dreyfus has generously provided me with a larger one of himself . . ."

Now she had the picture on the hook, and was able to stand back—still on the desk—and take a long appraising look. Much like the look Clouseau continued to take of her . . .

"You will find, monsieur," she said, straightening the portrait one last time, "that Paris can be a very political place."

"Ah yes," he said, with a sad shake of the head, "politics—where greed dons the mask of morality."

"That's good. Very good." Finally she turned her eyes on him. "Did *you* say that?"

Looking behind him, Clouseau said, "Why, yes . . . yes I did. I have not worked in the big city for some time, but I have lived . . . you know, the life."

"I'm sure you have."

"You are?"

"Oh yes, Monsieur Clouseau."

"Ah." Pride swelled in his chest. "So you have heard of me."

"I've seen your file." Lovely mouth twitching with amusement, she moved to the edge of the desk, as if it were a diving board, and held out a delicate palm. "Your hand?"

Heady with the scent of her Chanel, Clouseau swallowed. "You are confused, you poor young thing. That is *your* hand . . ."

"Indeed. But if you take it . . . with yours . . . you could help me down."

"Of course—but in your precarious position, mademoiselle . . . I think more than a simple hand is in order."

And he extended both arms.

The warmth of her brown eyes was matched by that of her smile. "You are a charming man, Monsieur Clouseau."

"You a discerning young woman, mademoiselle."

"My name is Nicole."

She lowered herself into his arms, but as he attempted to position himself in a gentlemanly way, Clouseau wound up with his head between her legs. Holding onto her, he staggered around with Nicole, doing an awkward—and yet, to Clouseau at least—strangely satisfying dance.

Already, Clouseau thought, her nyloned thighs hugging his face, *it is good to be in the City of Love* . . .

As Clouseau and the chief inspector's private secretary got to know each other in the outer office, an equally important meeting was under way in Charles Dreyfus's inner sanctum.

Very much in his element, Dreyfus had been

for half an hour holding court before an assembly of twelve ace detectives, the cream of the Sûreté crop. He had moved with a dancer's grace and a surgeon's precision from one massive crime-scene photo to another, making points and raising questions.

Right now, his audience of experts in rapt attention, he stood poised beside the blow-up of the victim's neck, from which extended the deadly dart.

"Coach Gluant was killed by a poisonous dart of Chinese origin," Dreyfus said. "This much we know. Though sophisticated in design, gentlemen, delivering as it did a poison so deadly death was immediate . . . this weapon was child's play to use—and could have been applied by hand from anyone within arm's reach . . . and that includes such notable suspects as Bizu the spurned player, Xania the estranged lover, as well as various players and staff members, not to mention fans and photographers . . ."

Dreyfus walked to his desk; eyes followed. He plucked a prop from a soda can he had left there to make a significant point.

"This is a simple drinking straw, gentlemen," he said, holding up the slender paper tube. "Available throughout the stadium, at concession stands all around—and yet such a simple straw could be our murder weapon."

A detective near the front of the several rows

lifted a hand and asked, "But surely not with much distance or accuracy, Chief Inspector."

"I beg to differ. Our forensics lab has already run a test confirming accuracy up to thirty feet . . . This expands our suspect list to everyone—from angry Chinese fans to any enemy from Gluant's past who might have a grudge, and a homicidal urge to act upon. And you don't reach a position like Gluant's without making enemies . . ."

Dreyfus whirled to Renard, who as always stood patiently on the periphery. "My deputy chief, Renard, here, will head a team analyzing all available television footage . . . identifying every person in the kill zone, targeting each for investigation." Then to Renard he said, "And you will swiftly carry out those investigations!"

Renard almost clicked his heels. "Yes, Chief Inspector!"

"You will also locate every firm in China making darts. And every firm both there and in the UK—export and import—dealing with those darts. We'll want their order books going back five years."

"It will be done."

Dreyfus turned to a sharp-eyed figure in the first row. "Corbeille? You are to put together Gluant's schedule going back as far as last year. Day by day. Everything he did."

"Yes, Chief Inspector. And if we find nothing of significance?"

"Go back *another* year! And another!" Dreyfus spun to a new position. "Savard!"

Another ace detective sat erect. "Yes, sir?"

"Your team will investigate anyone Gluant had dealings with—anyone he owed money to, anyone who had a grudge against him."

"Going back how far, Chief Inspector?"

Dreyfus's eyes flamed. "If he bullied a child in kindergarten, I want to know about it! And I want to know the whereabouts of that 'child' at the time of the murder! Is that clear?"

"As crystal, Chief Inspector."

"Good. Good." Dreyfus smiled. He rubbed his hands together like a hungry man about to sit before a feast. "I have confidence in you. You are the very best. Now . . . if you gentlemen will gather your things, and depart via the back way, I will meet with . . . the very worst."

The detectives—who had not been entrusted with the chief inspector's unconventional strategy—exchanged a few puzzled glances, but did as they were told, assembling their files and their notes, and departing quickly.

"Renard," Dreyfus said, "bring in this . . . this . . . what was his name again?"

"Clouseau?"

"Yes. Yes. Bring him to me."

Renard stepped into the outer office, where Clouseau and Nicole had wound up against a wall, the officer's head deep beneath her skirt, the young woman's lovely legs wrapped around his head.

"Clouseau?" Renard asked.

From beneath the dress came a muffled: "Ready for active duty, sir!"

Nicole offered the deputy a chagrined grin and a small shrug.

"I'm sure you are . . . the chief inspector will see you now."

By the time Renard returned to the office, only Dreyfus remained.

"Well . . . is he coming?" the chief inspector demanded.

Renard's mouth opened but nothing came out.

The chief inspector moved closer and asked, confidentially, "You needn't be circumspect with me, my dear Renard. Any first impressions about the man?"

"Well, sir . . ." Renard thought about it. "He would seem to have a way with the ladies."

And within moments, Dreyfus found himself looking at a striking military figure, perfection personified in a gendarme uniform, as if a picture on a Police Nationale recruiting poster had walked down off the wall to offer a crisp salute.

"Officer Jacques Clouseau, reporting! Gendarme Third Class!"

Dreyfus was just wondering if he'd made the right decision—surely, *this* was no boob!

And then Clouseau, with lightning speed, removed his wallet, flipped it open to display his badge . . .

. . . which flew across the room and impaled itself in Dreyfus's chest.

"Swine badge," Clouseau said, crossing to his superior officer. "We must write whoever it is who manufactures these defective items, putting our valiant force at risk . . . Sorry. That must have hurt."

"No," Dreyfus said, with a grimace, and withdrew the badge from his suitcoat—and his flesh—and handed it back to Clouseau, who deftly waved away the droplets of blood and returned the badge to his wallet. "The reason you've been called here—"

But Clouseau, his eyes large and suddenly darting, raised a hand in the manner of a traffic cop.

Dreyfus froze.

Clouseau began to wander around the office, looking here and there, ducking, weaving, bobbing, all the while saying, in a loud voice indeed, *"Such very pleasant weather we are having. I hope this blissful weather, she continues . . ."*

Dreyfus watched in amazement as Clouseau gestured frantically for him to join in on the inane conversation.

"Yes, yes," the chief inspector found himself saying, "the weather, she is . . . is blissful . . ."

Hugely pleased, Clouseau gestured thumbs up, and then quickly checked under a lamp, its shade flying and breaking the glass on a small framed picture of the President; then the gendarme lurched for a look behind a sofa, continuing his weather report as he moved on.

"If the clouds were any more white," Clouseau said, drawing back a curtain quickly, *"we might mistake them for snow . . . Is not that right, Chief Inspector?"*

"Yes, yes—snow . . ."

Clouseau snapped open the other curtain, and it fell to the floor in a pile.

Then the gendarme approached the chief inspector and whispered, "I believe we are secure."

"You do?"

"Yes . . . but as a final precaution, I suggest we speak the English."

"The . . . English?"

"Yes. You *do* speak the English, Chief Inspector?"

"I do. Yes."

"I am sure you know, from my file, that I am a master linguist. I speak eight or nine tongues. Sometimes I can't keep track myself, so many tongues do I have. So English?"

The chief inspector shrugged. "English. But Clouseau, all this fuss—you know, we are a sophisticated operation, here. We regularly sweep for bugs."

"And a wise precaution, too—these old buildings, the termite, she is a stern warden, no?"

Unable to summon a response, Dreyfus headed

behind his desk and sat, while Clouseau looked in puzzlement at the many chairs, and rather than select one, planted himself before his superior, at parade rest.

Clouseau said, "And why do you honor me with this meeting, Chief Inspector?"

Business-like, Dreyfus said, "Clouseau, I've reviewed your record, and it is in my considered opinion that you are . . . unique."

"Thank you, sir. I must humbly agree."

"I thought you might. Would you also agree that your talents merit greater responsibility than you've previously been given?"

"Wholeheartedly." A modest little smile twitched beneath the mustache. "I have often wondered how long it would take for the stories of my expertise to reach your desk."

"Well, reach my desk they have, Clouseau—and I am hereby promoting you to the high and honored rank of inspector."

"Inspector?" Clouseau swallowed; his eyes seemed about to tear up. "Of the Police Nationale? Of the Republic of France?"

Not sure what other option there might have been, Dreyfus said, "Yes. And perhaps you can guess what your first case will be . . ." The chief inspector half-smiled and gestured broadly to the huge crime scene blow-ups on easels all around.

Frowning in thought, Clouseau took in the looming photos with their grisly subject matter.

He began to stalk about the room, looking at each one in shock and horror.

"Who has done this terrible thing?" he demanded.

"That," the chief inspector said, "it is your job to find out."

"To . . . to clutter up the office of a great pubic servant such as yourself with such vile photos! We will find him, this madman! We will start with the photo labs, for it is within such labs that crimes of this magnitude are shaped!"

Frozen again, Dreyfus sat with his mouth open. Finally words came out, "No, no, Clouseau . . . *I* had these made. These are from the crime scene of the Gluant case."

Clouseau's eyes narrowed shrewdly. "The great soccer coach who was killed?"

"Yes."

"I have heard of this crime."

"Really."

Again Clouseau stood ramrod straight. "I would humbly volunteer to be assigned to that case!"

Dreyfus chuckled. "It is *yours* . . . Inspector Clouseau."

The very words seemed to rock him back. "Inspector . . . Clouseau . . . And yet . . . it has a ring to it, does it not?"

Dreyfus raised a finger. "But this is more than just a simple murder. This is two cases within one, and both are of key interest to France and her people. Finding Gluant's murderer is only the beginning—you must also solve the theft of the Pink Panther."

Clouseau's eyes showed white all round. "The famous stone? With its great legacy and aura of mystery?"

"Exactly."

Clouseau clicked his heels together. "I accept, Chief Inspector! I accept with honor."

Dreyfus stepped from behind the desk and presented Clouseau with a formal certificate bearing the state seal of France. "Jacques Clouseau—with the power vested in me, I hereby appoint you a full inspector of the Police Nationale."

With exaggerated ceremony, Dreyfus removed his gold fountain pen, and leaned over the side of his desk to sign the certificate with a flourish.

Dreyfus said, "All that is left, Inspector, is *your* signature . . ."

Clouseau patted himself, looking for a pen.

Dreyfus said, "Here. Take mine."

Clouseau took the gold pen and said, effusively, "Oh, Chief Inspector, you are too generous! Thank you! One does not often see the traditional French fountain pen."

The inspector signed the certificate, then began to study the pen with wide eyes, shaking it several times, hefting it, then putting it in his breast pocket.

"Chief Inspector, I will cherish this pen forever . . ."

"That was given to me by the mayor," Dreyfus said irritably.

Clouseau waved a hand. "Then I cannot accept this. But I will cherish the gesture."

The inspector graciously transferred the pen from his own pocket back to Dreyfus's.

The chief inspector suddenly felt woozy. He placed a hand over his face and muttered, "Where . . . where were we?"

"Well, I was here . . . I have not moved. You, I would I say, were perhaps . . . a few steps back. Why? What significance does this have?"

Renard materialized from the sidelines and said to the chief inspector, "Sir—the press conference?"

Dreyfus, unaware that a small ink stain on his suitcoat pocket was spreading into an ink blot reminiscent of those used by psychiatrists to test their patients, turned to Clouseau and said, "In a few minutes, we'll be presenting a press conference in the lobby. We want to properly introduce you to the media, and explain your key role in the Gluant investigation."

Clouseau (who *had* noticed the widening ink splotch) seemed anxious to leave. "Well, then, uh, I will meet you *down* there, Chief Inspector . . ."

Another man might have exited with no further ado. But Clouseau—as the chief inspector was soon to learn—could always find further ado to do. And now, as the new inspector backed out through the door, he took the time to point out the .elaborate filagree woodworking that surrounded the passage.

"So lovely!" Clouseau blurted, and reached around to put his hand against the woodworking. "One does not often see authentic eighteenth-century filigree. So finely done. Such workmanship. To think—it has been here for three hundred years! Our children's children will . . ."

And at this the filagree parted from the doorway and began unraveling, like a loose thread from a sweater that had been better left alone. The strips of wood clattered to the floor and Clouseau quickly gathered them up and stacked them against the wall.

"The magical thing," Clouseau said, with a smile as sick as Dreyfus felt, "is that it looks good anywhere."

Patting the exposed area where the filigree had been, Clouseau said, "Yes . . . yes, this area is secure."

And slipped out.

Alone with Renard, Dreyfus said, "I think we have found our man."

"Yes, sir. Indeed, sir."

"But perhaps I have succeeded too well."

"Sir?"

"I seem to be sweating . . . My chest . . . it's so damp . . ." Then he looked down at the black blotch and said, "My God, Renard!"

"Sorry, sir . . . I should have said something about—"

"Does it . . . does it look to you a little like—a cat chasing a dog?"

Renard swallowed. "I couldn't say, sir. Shall I get your spare suit?"

FOUR

Man of the Hour

Over the many years, in the elaborate lobby of the Palais de la Justice, countless press conferences had been held. But perhaps never had the anticipation among the press corps been so high, the murmuring of the normally blase, unflappable reporters echoing off the high-arched ceiling like gathering thunder.

Coach Gluant had been a national hero; the Pink Panther a national symbol.

How would the government deal with crimes that were, at their core, assaults upon France itself, contemptuous attacks on her national pride?

Speculation was high that Chief Inspector Dreyfus would personally come forward to lead the investigation; Dreyfus had a record second to none in a crime-fighting career that had a decade ago led him to his high office. Would he step away from his desk to take on this challenge himself?

As the reporters and TV crews surged before the platform, the gendarmes lining the walls trained alert eyes on the throng, as three men marched up onto the stage: Chief Inspector Dreyfus, his loyal Deputy Chief Renard, and a third individual, a man in a brown suit with a faintly provincial cut, and yet . . . many of the reporters sensed something special about this fellow, the jut of his chin, the oh-so French slash of mustache above a tightly confident smile, the eyes eternally narrowed in shrewd vigilance.

Who was this new player on the Parisian scene?

The chief inspector, stepping to the microphone, kept the media in suspense for only a few minutes, as he opened with a statement expressing the government's position on these heinous crimes, recognizing their importance and the need for immediate, decisive action.

"My staff searched the files of the Police Nationale," Dreyfus said, brows tensed, "and examined records of every officer assigned to investigative duties throughout all of France. We found, in the simple village of Fromage, a man whose record is so distinctive, so unusual in its accomplishments, that he could not be overlooked."

The eyes of the press corps—normally half-lidded in business-as-usual boredom—were wide, alert and keen.

Dreyfus gestured to the jauntily mustached man beside him. "And *this* is that man, brought in specifically to head up our investigation into these two interrelated crimes—*Inspector Jacques Clouseau!*"

The reporters began to shout their questions, thrusting forward microphones; but Dreyfus silenced them, patting the air with a cool palm, saying, "Gentlemen . . . ladies. You know the protocol. I understand this is a situation unlike any other in the history of crime in France. But we *will* maintain the civilities."

Then Dreyfus turned to Inspector Clouseau, and gestured to the microphone and, with a small bow, got out of the way of the man of the hour.

Clouseau looked out into the audience and immediately noticed a female reporter who was no more attractive than, say, the young Brigitte Bardot, and who admirably filled a tube top that rose slightly, exposing the lower swells of white flesh, when she raised a hand to seek recognition.

The inspector rewarded her with the first question.

"Parisian *Match*, Inspector Clouseau," she said. "To be singled out from all of France to head this inquiry is a huge honor. Do you have your own unique method of investigation, Inspector, that has brought you to this rarefied position?"

"I do, Mademoiselle Match, I do indeed. I start with the initial premise, and from this I deduce certain other facts." He gestured with both hands, smiled tightly, as if this answered all. "Are there any other questions?"

Clouseau's eyes roamed the crowd, as hands raised high, in keeping with the protocol Dreyfus had invoked; the inspector, seeking another questioner, landed upon . . .

. . . the same young woman, who alone in the room had not raised her hand, having been selected already.

Clouseau smiled at her. "Did you have another question?"

"Well. Uh, yes. Certainly. Inspector, what—"

"No! No, I am sorry, my dear. As my esteemed superior has pointed out, we are a society of rules. Of law."

In the confused crowd of reporters, she was the most confused of all.

"I must insist," Clouseau said, "that you raise your hand in keeping with protocol."

She did.

Clouseau smiled, sighed to himself, then nodded to her. "Yes?"

"This particular case—what *is* the initial premise?"

"Excellent question! An excellent question. We

begin at the beginning . . . which is that Gluant, he did not wish to be killed. And from this flows all else, like mercury down the gently sloping . . . slopes . . . of the swelling . . . slopes. Did you have a follow-up question, Ms. Match?"

"Yes, Inspector. How—"

"But I must insist . . . These rules, I don't make them, but without them, where would we be?"

She raised her hand.

Clouseau seemed lost in dreamy thought.

Dreyfus poked him.

"*Yes*, my dear," Clouseau said. "Your follow-up?"

"How long do you think it will take you to find the killer?"

"Well, first we must identify the killer. Only when we have identified the killer are we able to find the killer. And when we find the killer . . . and here is where my unique methods come into play . . . we must *trap* the killer. Did you have another follow-up . . . ?"

The female reporter shrugged her bare shoulders.

"Please, please . . . protocol."

Sighing, she raised her hand. "*How* will you trap the killer?"

"Two points come to mind."

But he was just staring at her.

Dreyfus prodded him again, and Clouseau blurted, "*First*—first, you must remember that we have the killer surrounded right now by a web of deduction, forensic science and the latest in technology. We have the test tube, we have the two-way radio, we have the crime scene tape . . . bright yellow."

Again, dutifully raising her hand, the *Match* reporter asked, "And the *other* point?"

Clouseau's brow knit. "The other point?"

"You said there were *two* points."

"Ah yes. But right now I cannot put my finger on it."

Behind Clouseau, Chief Inspector Charles Dreyfus was beginning to wonder what exactly he had unleashed upon his beloved Paris. He took Renard by the arm, and drew him near, whispering, "Assign a fool to this man."

"You mean—assign a man to this fool?"

Dreyfus shook his head, half expecting his eyes to rattle. "Yes. Yes, of course."

"To do what, Chief Inspector?"

"To be his driver . . . and report on his whereabouts."

"What kind of a man, Chief Inspector?"

"The kind that follows orders, and does not ask questions . . . Any questions?"

"Uh, no, sir."

Then, with a confident expression, Clouseau asked, "Are there any foreign press present? I speak the ten tongues."

"*New York Times!*" a male reporter called out in

English. "Do you know if the killer was a man or a woman?"

"Of course I know it is a man or a woman!" Clouseau spat back in English. "What else would it be—a kitten?" He nodded to another reporter.

"*Newsweek*, Inspector—do you think it is possible that the killer could be watching you right now?"

Clouseau narrowed his eyes until they were almost closed; he began to nod, slowly. "This is a very good possibility." His gaze returned to the female reporter. "The strip search of the press, it is something unorthodox that you suggest, but—"

The American reporter said, "No, I meant, do you think the killer is watching you on the *television* right now?"

"Where else would he watch—the radio?" Clouseau shook his head at such foolishness, then his expression shifted, dead serious. One eye closed, another widened. "He may be watching, yes. Or he may be taping, the time-delay ploy. It is, after all, not every day one is talked about on the TV. It is, in my opinion, one of the real benefits for the mad killer. For that reason, I have a personal massage for the killer!"

"A massage?" the reporter asked.

"A massage! A *massage*!" Then Clouseau sought out the nearest camera and spoke directly to it, in his native tongue: "There is no place you can hide—no place you cannot be seen by the all-seeing eyes of Inspector Jacques Clouseau, which see all things in their . . . sight! To *you* killer, I say—*I will find you!*"

The inspector's delivery was spellbinding; the press corps seemed in rapture—a pin could have dropped, and if Clouseau had had one, it probably would have.

"And *why*, do you ask, will Clouseau do this thing?" The great detective continued, straightening up, saying, "Because I am a servant of our great nation . . ." His voice built. ". . . because justice is justice . . ." He raised a fist. ". . . and because France . . . is *France!*"

The inspector beat his chest with his fist hurting himself, but just a little, and saluted the press corps. The hardboiled reporters, caught up perhaps in the importance of the Pink Panther crisis, were enthralled with this new star—the inspector appeared coolly confident, a touch eccentric perhaps, but incredibly determined . . . and oh so very French . . .

Flashbulbs popped, and those gendarmes who had been as silent as dark blue curtains against the walls exploded into cheers and applause.

Dreyfus—the flashbulbs triggering a tiny twitch at his left eye—asked, "What have I done, Renard?"

"You've given France a new hero, sir. Who just happens to be the biggest fool on the face of the earth." Renard shrugged. "Not just any man could have managed that, sir . . ."

Inspector Jacques Clouseau stepped into the office.

While not lavish—certainly nothing to compare with the chief inspector's—the spacious room was a far cry from a simple cubicle in the bullpen of gendarmes at the rural headquarters in Fromage.

Nicole, lovely in short-skirted blue again, stood next to a rather massive wooden desk, on which were piled file after file.

"Bon jour, Nicole," he said, his eyes still traveling around the room.

She adjusted her glasses on her pert nose and smiled. "Your new office—how do you like it?"

"It will suffice. It will suffice."

She gestured toward the desktop. "You should probably start by going through these files—"

Clouseau held up his palm and shook his head, shushing her.

He began to inspect the room, checking behind curtains, and inside the shade of the desk lamp; taking a closer look at the latter, he found something suspicious. Raising his voice, he said, "*Such very pleasant weather we are having,* bon? *She is blissful, this weather . . . is she not?*"

Nicole frowned in confusion.

He whispered, "Be natural . . ." Then he said,

almost shouting, *"If the clouds were any more white, we might mistake them for snow . . . no?"*

"N-no," Nicole said.

Again he whispered to her, almost inaudibly, "I check for the electronic listening device . . . what the Americans call 'the boog.' "

"The boog?"

He shushed her, then—with a slightly maniacal expression—he pulled a length of wire from within the lamp with one hand, as with the other he removed his Swiss Army knife from a pants pocket.

"I hope," he almost shouted, *"the weather, she stays this pleasant . . . Do you not agree?"*

With the bare blade, he began to cut the cord.

The sizzle of electricity shook him like a naughty child, the lightbulb went out, and the scent of soot wafted through the air.

Tiny trails of smoke rose from his body, and his white hair seemed to stand up a little, rather punkishly Nicole thought. His mustache had a new rakish tilt. He let out a deep breath, uncrossed his eyes, smoothed his suit, and granted her an efficient nod.

"The area," he said, "she is secure."

He wandered about the office, admiring the built-in bookcases with their numerous legal volumes and attractive knickknacks. In particular he was pleased with the large globe near the window—a fine touch, Clouseau thought, an indication that the entire world was now his beat. He strolled over for a closer look, and idly began to spin the globe as he spoke to the chief inspector's secretary.

"The world, Nicole . . . a dangerous place. It requires . . . supervision, do you not agree?"

"Uh, yes, Inspector." She again gestured to the work piled on the desk. "When you've gone over these files, I will bring you more files."

"And where," Clouseau said, idly spinning the globe, faster, faster, "are these files filed?"

"I file them in the filing cabinet."

"Ah."

"I will refile these files, when—"

And the globe spun off its stand and rolled past Nicole, who watched with wide eyes as the world made its way out the open office door.

They could hear it clunking noisily down the stairs, one step at a time, like a child's ball. But bigger.

And heavier.

Then Nicole joined Clouseau at the window, where he was watching as the globe rolled down the outer marble steps of the magnificent building. He opened the glass and leaned out, as did she, taking in the sight of the large globe making its way down the busy street, between lanes.

"That globe," she said breathlessly.

"Yes. That is a globe."

"It was a hundred years old!"

"Ah. What a relief that is to hear." He withdrew from the window. "I admit feeling concern—to have ruined a new globe, well . . . This is what these fools who dress these offices get!"

She blinked at him. "It is?"

"Here I am heading up the most important investigation in all of France, and they decorate my office with a second-hand globe? I will write to those in charge."

Nicole nodded, having no idea who that might be.

Clouseau was behind his desk now, trying out the swivel chair. When he picked himself back up off the floor ("Swine chair!"), he sat again, and he looked with narrow eyes at the desk drawers. He gave Nicole a knowing little smile, and she watched in fascination as the inspector plucked a hair from his head and wedged it in his top desk drawer.

"A precaution of the safety," he said.

"Hmmm. Good idea. Uh, Inspector, you will need new clothes."

"You do not like my clothes?"

"It's not that. You have charming taste, Inspector. But in your high-ranking office, several new suits come with the job."

The eyes narrowed further. "Suppose I am of a different size than the previous inspector?"

She moved around behind the desk with him.

"No, these will be tailored specifically for your needs. That's why I can . . . if you like . . . take your measurements. Then you'll have a perfect fit."

"Nicole, my temper, I never lose it. I am in full control of my—"

"I mean, for the tailor. To make your new clothes." She reached out a hand. "Your coat?"

"Yes, this is my coat."

"Take it off so I can measure you."

"Ah—should I stand?"

"Not necessary."

He got out of his coat and handed it to her, and she lay it on the desk; then she withdrew a tape measure from her sweater pocket and began with his extended arms. Their proximity unnerved them both. Nicole found herself strangely attracted to this odd character; or perhaps she was oddly attracted to this strange character—she could not be sure.

She was measuring his left arm when she heard herself say, "Do you . . . live by yourself, Inspector?"

"Yes, yes. It is a lonely life, the servant of the public, the solver of the crimes."

Their eyes locked. "You *do* get lonely, then?"

"Not so much. I am the reader voracious."

"Ah! Novels? Nonfiction?"

"Internet."

Kneeling before him, she found herself facing

his belt buckle. She began to gently slide the tape measure up his thigh and beyond.

"My," she said. "You do have a long in-seam."

"Thank you."

"Perhaps you could loosen your belt . . . so I can measure your waist?"

"Of course . . ."

And he unbuckled his belt.

"That doesn't quite do it." She gave him an apologetic smile. "Would you mind, Inspector . . . ?"

"Not at all," he said, and unzipped his fly.

Following orders, which was something at which he was most adept, Detective Second Class Gilbert Ponton approached the office of the newest inspector of the Police Nationale. He glanced at the freshly painted INSPECTOR JACQUES CLOUSEAU on the glass of a door that stood open, and reached a huge paw in, to knock.

At six foot four, Ponton was perhaps the tallest, and certainly one of the beefiest, plainclothes officers on the force. He was not the most imaginative policeman in Paris, nor the most brilliant, but he was loyal, and dogged. And he had been selected to do a job for the chief inspector himself, which was a compliment, however uncomfortable Ponton might feel about the ethics of the assignment.

Oval-faced, with a small mustache, half-lidded

eyes and the simple manner of a peasant, Ponton knew only that he was expected to report back to the deputy chief on the progress of Inspector Clouseau's investigation into the Gluant murder and the Pink Panther theft.

That he, Gilbert Ponton, would be included as any small part of so important a case pleased the humble detective; but he felt awkward about pairing up with a partner—who after all had been handpicked to head up this important investigation—only to secretly "keep an eye on the fool," as Chief Deputy Renard had put it.

How strange for Renard to speak so disrespectfully of the detective selected from all detectives to handle the investigation of all investigations . . .

But his was not to reason why. His was to knock on Inspector Clouseau's door.

Which he did.

And a firm, confident voice called, "Come!"

Ponton stuck his head in. "I may be a little early. My appointment is—"

"You will find that Jacques Clouseau does not stand on ceremony!" In fact Clouseau wasn't standing at all—he was seated behind an impressive desk, somewhat sideways, his back somewhat to his unexpected guest.

Ponton shuffled in, moving toward the visitor's chair opposite Clouseau, when he noticed the lovely female legs sticking out from behind . . . from under . . . the side of the desk where Clouseau sat.

Hovering awkwardly, Ponton said, "I . . . I can come back in a few minutes if—"

"Nonsense! We'll be done in a shake of the lamb's tail."

Shrugging to himself as much as to his host, Ponton took his seat. A moment later, he heard a clearing of the throat, and a beautiful young woman stood, and straightened her skirt and her eyeglasses.

"There," she said. "That takes care of that— and welcome to Paris, Inspector Clouseau."

Clouseau nodded to her. "Thank you, Nicole. You are most kind."

The lovely young woman nodded to Ponton as she exited. Ponton watched her go, in amazed appreciation.

"Is . . . is that your secretary, Inspector?"

"No, no—she is the chief inspector's. She stopped by to service my needs, as a matter of courtesy. You know, I have transferred in from the country, and I must say I am, as the Americans say, 'blown away' by the warm welcome provided to a newcomer like myself."

Ponton nodded, glancing in the direction in which the woman had disappeared. "It is . . . impressive. I have worked in a precinct for some years where the secretaries are not really so friendly."

"I apologize for the wait, but I have just arrived at my office, and I admit to not yet checking the calendar of my appointments." Clouseau began looking around the desk for it, moving files aside. "I am afraid I was somewhat distracted . . ."

"Who could blame you?"

"Ah, here it is!" Clouseau held up the appointment calendar, whapped the small book against a palm, and then put it away in the desk. He folded his hands and beamed at his guest. "And you are . . . ?"

"Ponton—Gilbert. Detective Second Class."

"Ah, Ponton Gilbert. And what is your assignment?"

"It's . . . Gilbert Ponton."

Clouseau nodded, eyes tightening. "And how long have you been assigned to watch this fellow?"

"What fellow?"

"Gilbert Ponton!"

"That's . . . that's my name."

"An amazing coincidence. But I suspect all coincidences, and I suggest you do the same. And what bearing might this have on the Gluant case, Detective Ponton?"

"I have been assigned to assist you."

"Ah." Clouseau nodded. Then his eyes took on an appraising cast. "And what qualifications do you have for police work?"

Ponton stiffened proudly. "My family has performed police work in Paris for nine generations!"

"I see. And before that?"

"Well . . . we were policemen in the surrounding areas for two hundred years."

A curt nod from Clouseau. "And before that?"

"My ancestors were immigrants . . . from various countries around Europe . . . always involved in keeping the peace."

"I see. And before that?"

"I . . . I honestly don't know."

Clouseau chuckled, and waved off this information. "And so they send you, the novice, the innocent lamb, for Clouseau to teach. Ponton Gilbert—"

"Gilbert Ponton."

The inspector stood and his pants fell, gathering at his knees. "My large friend, I vow to teach you everything I know about the police science . . . and the investigator's art. I have been the mentor to many over the years. But none . . . not one of them . . . was as tall as you."

Ponton's eyebrows rose. "Thank you . . . ?"

Pulling his trousers into place, zipping up and rebuckling his belt, he said, "You are most welcome, my large protege. And where do you think we will begin, Gilbert Ponton Ponton Gilbert?"

"At the beginning?"

"Yes! Yes! At the beginning . . . for that is where we are." Clouseau pointed dramatically at his new partner. "The beginning of catching a killer!"

FIVE

The Perfect Suspect

Within his expansive, well-appointed office, Chief Inspector Dreyfus—attended as always by Chief Deputy Renard—met with several of the real investigators on the case, including the coldly handsome Detective Corbeille. While Clouseau led himself—and the media—on a merry chase, Dreyfus would guide the true leading lights of French criminology on the search for the Pink Panther . . . and the killer of Coach Gluant; that was important, too . . .

Right now Dreyfus was reviewing key video footage, on the monitor screen a close-up of Gluant and his star forward, the blond boyish Jacquard, embracing after the latter's winning goal. Just as they were being swarmed by enthusiastic fans, staffers and teammates, Dreyfus commanded Renard to freeze the frame.

With a pointer Dreyfus tapped the glass, the tip indicating various angry Chinese faces in the screen's upper corner.

"This, of course, is the Chinese VIP box," Dreyfus said to the investigators, their eyes affixed to the glowing image. "They are positioned right at the edge of what our forensics experts have labeled the 'kill zone.' "

Wandering away from the screen, meeting the eyes of each of the detectives, Dreyfus slowly paced before them, his manner cool, professional and—as with any great detective—probing.

"The poison was Chinese," he said, planting himself before Corbeille. "Do we know if Gluant ever took a team to China, or was in any other way a visitor to that country?"

Corbeille, as able as Clouseau was bumbling, nodded sagely, arms folded. "Three years ago."

"The occasion?"

"He took a group of French stars there—exhibition games. Cultural goodwill."

"Like the 'goodwill' that struck him down on the sidelines of a French football victory, eh?" Dreyfus smiled with bitter satisfaction. "Gentlemen, I do not claim to know for certain—it is too early for that—but the facts conspire with my investigative instincts to send me looking in the direction of our Chinese 'friends.' "

Nods all around.

Dreyfus thrust a finger at Corbeille. "Get on the next flight to Beijing! Find out what Gluant did there—on every day of his visit, a minute-by-minute account."

"Yes, sir. At once, Chief Inspector."

Then he whirled to Detective Pacquette, an investigator as brilliant as Clouseau was dimwitted. "Have we identified everyone in the Chinese VIP box—from dignitaries to bodyguards to minor functionaries?"

"Actually, we have, Chief Inspector."

"Excellent!" His face hardened. "Now—build me a dossier on each and every one of them. Go! All of you! Time is our enemy."

And the detectives went—quickly, the force of Dreyfus's personality compelling them to do their best, and right away.

Renard, again materializing like a friendly ghost at the chief inspector's side, said, "We have our first report in from Ponton. He has made contact with Clouseau."

"Excellent."

"He indicates Clouseau has accepted him as a protege. Taken him on as . . . a pupil."

Dreyfus frowned. "But Ponton has been on the Police Nationale at *least* as long as Clouseau!"

A tiny shrug. "It would appear Clouseau's incompetence is matched only by his inflated ego."

Dreyfus nodded. "Sad, is it not, Renard? When a well-meaning public servant allows his own ego to swell to such dangerous proportions?"

Renard, whose mind immediately had gone to the enormous new portrait of Dreyfus hanging in the outer office, did not reply at once.

Finally, he said, "Yes, Chief Inspector. It can be . . . dangerous indeed."

On a bustling street in a Parisian square, Inspector Clouseau—who after all was a plainclothes officer now—endeavored not to be overly conspicuous. Toward that end he gestured only occasionally with his riding crop.

He looked up at this poor simple child of a man, Ponton, who had been assigned to him, as a baby is assigned to a nanny. Such simple features—Clouseau wondered if a man of such obviously average intelligence could hope to succeed in the world of criminal investigation.

The great detective would do his best for his charge.

Eyeing his hulking partner doubtfully as they walked along, Clouseau said, "I am concerned for your welfare, my large friend. You have risen only to the rank of detective second class, whereas I, Jacques Clouseau, have achieved the status of inspector!"

Ponton nodded. "Yes. Since yesterday, wasn't it?"

"Yesterday—after a lifetime of hard work and the sharp deductive skill. If I may be frank?"

"Please."

"Your senses do not appear to be as finely honed as my own. Ah, it is nothing to feel ashamed about! . . . But even one who is not born with such gifts may acquire them through diligence and practice, practice, practice. Ow, ow, ow."

"What do you have in mind, Inspector?"

Clouseau paused, tripping a mustached man in a beret carrying a baguette. The detective said, "Watch where you are going, you fool!"

The man in the beret, picking himself and his bread up, said in English, "I'm sorry—I don't speak French," and moved on.

Clouseau watched him go, shook his head, and returned his attention to his charge. "Detective Ponton, I have in mind a plan, a plan so simple in its elegance that is . . . how shall I put it? Simply elegant."

"What is that plan, Inspector?"

Clouseau raised a conspiratorial forefinger and smiled a sly smile as he leaned in. "Intermittently—and without warning—I will *attack* you! Whenever and wherever it is least expected . . . it may be night! It may be day! Vigilance, my large friend. Vigilance . . . but I must warn you:

Clouseau, he holds the black belt in the arts martiale."

Ponton shrugged. "All right."

Clouseau gestured in an openhanded friendly manner. "Shall we go?"

Ponton nodded, and walked on, Clouseau lagging half a step—and raised a hand in the deadly blade that his karate training had fashioned from flesh and bone . . .

Casually, Ponton swung back a fist and caught Clouseau in the face.

The inspector dropped to the pavement, then sprang to his feet, saying, "Excellent! I applaud you, Ponton. You are learning already."

Soon the pair had arrived at a nondescript brick building with a sign labeling it "Altermondial Recording Studios." After quickly checking the address with the one in the file Nicole had provided, Clouseau led his large assistant into the building where, up an elevator, they arrived at a doorway above which flashed a red light.

A sign said: DO NOT OPEN DOOR WHEN LIGHT IS FLASHING.

Clouseau eyed this shrewdly. Then, poised as a child waiting for the correct moment to leap onto a moving carousel, he waited between flashes and thrust himself through the door, making no more noise than he might have falling down a flight of stairs.

Ponton quietly followed.

The two detectives found themselves in an enormous, high-ceilinged, state-of-the-art studio, the floor of which was largely filled, wall to wall, by an orchestra playing a ballad, the strings executing a lovely melodic line. Beyond the several dozen musicians, lost in their work, an isolation booth could be seen, where the beautiful diva Xania, in a gold-lame curve-hugging outfit, sang before a microphone, in headphones. Though her lips moved, her voice could not be heard in the studio.

Clouseau whispered to Ponton, "They are making the music—this is their work, my inexperienced colleague; we must be unobtrusive, we must respect them in their creativity, and be silent as the mouse."

Ponton nodded.

Riding crop in hand, Clouseau began to work his way through the musicians, squeezing between them, finding aisles between rows, and nearly losing his balance. Waving his hand and the crop in an attempt to regain his footing, Clouseau came into the view of the conductor, on his small platform; as the detective and his large shadow wound awkwardly through the orchestra, that riding crop waving, the conductor's attention became glued to his visitors, and the tempo of the inspector's arm movements began to influence the conductor's own.

At the same time, various musicians found

themselves hypnotized by the clumsy poetry of Clouseau's movements, and his waving riding crop, and yet another tempo was achieved. And by the time Clouseau and his partner had snaked their way to the front of the studio, the lovely music had devolved into an aural train wreck.

Clouseau again whispered to his partner, "Perhaps these players, they are not as professional as we had thought. I believe I perceived a shift in tempo, and perhaps a wrong note."

"Perhaps," Ponton granted.

Clouseau stood before the glass behind which Xania valiantly continued singing; her mouth moved but her vocals remained inaudible in the studio.

Sotto voce, Clouseau confided in Ponton: "She speaks to me, but I cannot understand, over the caterwauling of these so-called musicians. And the lip reading, it is not, I am not proud to say, among the many talents of Clouseau."

"Ah," Ponton said.

"So when the Mohammed will not come to the molehill, the mountain, he will come to the . . . I will go to her. Stay here. Keep an eye on this orchestra."

"You suspect the orchestra?"

"I suspect *everyone*! And—I suspect *no* one."

Then he slipped into the booth, and—after a studied while—realized Xania was not speaking to him, rather singing. She broke off and said, just a little irritably, "Excuse me—I'm recording, here."

"That is all right," Clouseau said, and from his suitcoat pocket he revealed a small tape recorder. "So am I. I am Inspector Clouseau of the Police Nationale."

Her expression warmed up. "Well . . . hello, Inspector. I am Xania."

She held out her hand. He took her fingertips in his, and kissed the back of his own hand.

Then he released his grip and moved closer. "I am familiar with you and your work—one might say, intimately."

Beyond the isolation booth, the glass of the control room could be seen, a particularly agitated individual—the producer—was coming out, heading toward them through the seated musicians.

"Excuse me, Inspector," Xania said, and she emerged from the booth, calling, "It's all right, Roland! It's the Gluant case—these men are police!"

Joining her outside the isolation booth, the detective resumed his conversation with the diva. Xania regarded him with interest and mild amusement, while Clouseau attempted his most suave manner.

She said, "You say you are . . . *intimately* familiar with my work?"

Shyly he responded, "Well—let us just say that

I have memorized your finest artistic achievement."

"Really? Which CD do you mean?"

"I love them all. But I was referring to your swimsuit calendar."

She laughed lightly. "I find that touching."

"As do I. Almost every night."

She lay her cool palm against his warm cheek. "You are so very kind, Inspector. If only all of my fans were as sensitive and considerate as you."

"Thank you . . . This booth, it is the booth soundproof?"

"Yes."

"Would you wait here a moment? My mind is ever seeking new information, thirsting, hungering for knowledge. I would like to examine this . . . this soundproof booth, for the future reference."

She shrugged a little. "Why, certainly, Inspector . . ."

Clouseau stepped into the booth, his keen eyes taking in the many microphones, and the soundproof tile of the walls and ceiling. Then he paused and passed gas.

The rippling sound reverberated throughout the studio with no more force than Mount St. Helens erupting.

Stepping suavely from the booth, Clouseau discovered his assistant had taken the initiative to begin the questioning of the lovely suspect, who for some strange reason now regarded the inspector with a peculiar expression.

Ponton was asking, "You were nearby when Gluant was killed, Ms. Xania?"

"Just 'Xania' . . . yes, I ran out to be with him, to celebrate his team's victory. A tragedy most—"

"Tragique," Clouseau said.

"Yes," she said, with a grave little nod.

Clouseau picked up Ponton's interrogation—gently. "Now a few hours prior to the unfortunate event . . ."

"The murder," Ponton said.

Clouseau shot his assistant a look. "To the murder . . . six witnesses saw you and Coach Gluant together."

"That may be possible, Inspector."

"Apparently you and the deceased were having the conversation most animated . . . What was it exactly, Ponton?"

The assistant, referring to his notebook, said, "She was striking him repeatedly and screaming, 'You bastard! I'm going to kill you! I'm going to kill your cheating ass!' "

"I hope you will understand," Clouseau said, "that to some this might seem . . . somewhat suspicious."

She gestured with open hands—and open eyes. Lovely, deep brown, open eyes. "You're a man, Inspector. You know the ways of love . . ."

Clouseau's smile twitched under his mustache, which also twitched. "Well . . ."

"I was angry! I'd caught Gluant with another woman. And this was after he'd said he *loved* me—that he wanted me to *marry* him!"

"Swine murder victim," Clouseau said.

"And I *believed* him. I even gave him . . . the ultimate gift."

"Your swimsuit calendar?"

"My . . ." The sophisticated diva lowered her head shyly. ". . . my virginity."

Several members of the orchestra nearby dropped their instruments, and a few others coughed loudly. Even Ponton regarded her with arched eyebrows of skepticism, and the producer stifled a laugh.

But Clouseau took her small sweet hand in his (which was larger and less sweet) and said, "You are a poor dear little angel waif."

"Thank you, Inspector." She batted long lashes at him. "I just knew you'd understand."

"This, this, this is just an *expression*! How often have I heard people say to me, 'I'm going to kill you! I should kill you, you stupid fool!' This expression—is any expression so commonplace as this?"

A tear trickled down a perfect cheek. "When he cheated on me, I hated him."

"Of course you did, my child."

"But I didn't kill him."

"Of course you did not."

Ponton frowned and scratched his head. "Mademoiselle, did you recently perform in China? In a concert at—"

Clouseau's eyes and nostrils flared as he turned to his assistant. "Ponton, stop this incessant browbeating of this poor child! Can you not see she is distraught? That she needs the sexual healing?"

Xania said to Ponton, "I did perform a concert in Shanghai—three months ago. But what of that? I perform all over the world."

"Ponton!" Clouseau said, glaring. "Do you not recognize big talents when you see them! . . . My pet, do you know of anyone else who expressed hatred for the Coach Gluant?"

Her perfect face grew thoughtful. "He did have an abrasive side. He climbed to the top of his profession, after all. But if I were to single out one person, it would be his former star player—Bizu."

"God bless you," Clouseau said.

Ponton said, "She didn't sneeze, Inspector—she means the star forward, Bizu."

"I know what she means! Do not tell me what she means! . . . Xania, my sweet unsuspected one, can you tell me what is the basis for this Bizu's hostility toward Gluant?"

"I'm afraid *I* was the basis—I'd been dating Bizu when I became interested in Gluant, and he

81

in me. Bizu is such a child! And so possessive. He hated Gluant for 'stealing me away'—Bizu could not accept that I left him of my own free will. He needed someone to blame—and that was Gluant."

A voice from behind Clouseau said, "If you ask me, both Bizu and Gluant were no-good bastards."

Clouseau spun to face a slender dark-haired individual in sweater and slacks. "I do *not* ask you! . . . Who are you, the intruder who has sneaked into this studio to pry into my case?"

"I'm Xania's producer."

"And do you have a name?"

"Yes."

Clouseau thought about that, then thrust a finger at the producer and said, "You! You will not leave town!"

"But I'm flying to Montserrat tonight," he said, "to record Rene Duchanel—it's been booked for months!"

"Nonetheless, you will not leave town. This is a serious murder. And I may wish to ask you a few more questions."

The producer's features clenched in exasperation. "But I don't *know* anything!"

"About life? Perhaps not. About love? Surely nothing. But about this *crime*? You may hold the key!"

"Inspector, I barely even knew—"

"Do not leave Paris!" He spun to Ponton. "None of the key suspect are to leave the city! Clouseau has spoken."

Xania sidled seductively up next to the inspector. "But, Inspector—does that include me? Next week I have . . . something or other to do in New York."

He took her hand, gazed into the depths of her eyes. "My sweet, how could I stand in the way of something as important as that? Of course, you should feel free to go where you wish, as long as you let us know."

The producer said, "Well, in that case, Inspector—"

He rotated to the producer. "You will not leave town!" Then he returned to the beautiful diva and said, "You must place your trust in Clouseau, my dear Xania."

"How can I ever repay you, Inspector?"

He leaned close. "Perhaps, my sweet—one day, one Parisian night? You may lose your virginity to Jacques Clouseau, as well."

Her smile was so innocent and yet so wicked.

"Perhaps," she said.

SIX

Practice for Murder

The training facility of Team France required a drive to the suburbs, where Inspector Clouseau deposited his Renault in a parking lot in the shadow of the towering ultra-modern building. Looming was the team's famous logo, mounted next to an International Championship insignia.

"Most impressive," Ponton said, leaning out the car window.

Clouseau shut off the engine. "Thank you. But parking has been a specialty of mine for many years—you needn't comment on that again. It would only embarrass me."

Ponton said, "I will restrain myself."

The large man took the lead, heading up the

steps. Clouseau, smiling devilishly, mustache atwitch, came up quickly behind his pupil. Barely turning, Ponton parried the karate chop and caught Clouseau by the tie before he fell down the short flight.

"Are you all right, Inspector?"

"Of course I am all right!" His arms wind-milled as he regained his footing. "I am merely . . . moved by the progress you are making, my large friend." They were at the landing now. "Allow me . . ."

Clouseau opened the door and slammed it into Ponton, who tumbled backward down the steps.

The big man seemed only mildly dazed as Clouseau helped him to his feet. "Ah, but my enormous colleague, you must maintain the vigilance. The vigilance!"

Shortly, within the facility, the receptionist directed the detectives to Cherie Dubois, the team's publicity person. An attractive, athletic-looking blonde in her twenties, wearing a Team France t-shirt and short skirt, she accompanied the men down the corridor.

"I'm afraid, Inspector," she said, "I cannot take you to see Bizu."

"Ah, but mademoiselle—there is no need to be afraid. Jacques Clouseau will protect you from this beast."

"No, you . . . you don't understand. Monsieur Bizu is unavailable at the moment. But I can take you to see Monsieur Vainqueur—he *was* the assistant coach . . . he is the new head coach, now."

Clouseau seemed confused. "He . . . coaches the head? Is this really necessary? Most Frenchmen need no coaching in such—"

Ponton cleared his throat.

Clouseau gave his partner a look that seemed to say, *What?*

Cherie studied the inspector for a moment, and after spending several moments searching his eyes for intelligence, she gave up and said, "What I meant was, with Coach Gluant gone, Monsieur Vainqueur is the *main* coach."

"Oh! Oh, I see."

She stopped at a door and began to open it for them, but the inspector insisted that he be allowed to do her the honor.

With a gracious smile and nod, she stepped inside, while the gentlemanly Clouseau made a sweeping after-you gesture for Ponton, as well. The big man followed Clouseau, while Clouseau backed up to get a running start at him, and—karate-blade hands extended—he charged Ponton, who moved neatly aside, sending Clouseau flying into a practice net, which held him momentarily—a fly in its web—and sprang back to deposit him at Cherie's feet.

The inspector stood, brushing himself off, laughing in a forced manner, "My oversized companion and I, we have the . . . what is the expression? The joke that runs. I hope you do not mind."

Cherie said, "Not at all, Inspector."

To Clouseau she seemed vaguely amused; he wondered what secret knowledge lay behind this strange attitude.

She was saying, "You know, Inspector Clouseau, I've never met a policeman like you before."

"You are too generous, my child."

Clouseau allowed Ponton and Cherie to take the lead as they made their way along the side of the gym, cluttered as it was with workout equipment, soccer balls and practice nets, a few players practicing or exercising here and there.

Ponton said to Cherie, "Have you worked here long, Mademoiselle Dubois?"

"Yes, for almost two years."

"How did one so young come to be the team's public relations representative?"

"Monsieur Gluant hired me," she said, as if this answered Ponton's question.

"Were you and he close?"

"Well . . . we worked closely, you would say."

"Very closely?"

"Yes. Coach Gluant and I, we scouted players all over the world—our current trainer we hired away from the Russian military team, for example."

Clouseau, his timing as precise as any athlete in the vast room, made his move.

He ran toward Ponton's back, his deadly karate-chop hand poised; he would normally have pulled back on the blow, but Ponton could handle the full force, hulking brute that he was. With all of his considerable strength, Clouseau brought down the blade of his hand . . .

. . . against a chin-up bar.

The *whang* resounded, and Ponton and Cherie glanced back.

Clouseau patted the bar—with his other hand—and in an ear-to-ear smile that went well with his eyes . . . which seemed to be so happy that tears welled . . . the inspector said, "Ponton, make a note!"

"Yes, Inspector," the big man said, and got out his little pad.

"We must write those in charge and commend them for the strength of the steel in this equipment! Too often you come upon shoddy workmanship, but not here, at the Team France training facility. I salute you, makers of this steel."

And the inspector actually did salute, putting his other hand in contact with the chin-up bar, making only a *clang* this time.

Ponton asked the young woman, "If you worked this closely with the coach, did this inspire jealousy in other women? Xania, perhaps?"

"*What* other women?"

Ponton's eyebrows raised. "You mean . . . Xania was the only one . . . ?"

She let out a wicked laugh. "Xania! Don't believe everything you read in the papers, Detective Ponton. I can tell you with utter certainty that Coach Gluant was *finished* with her—*through!*"

Clouseau caught up with them, asking, "Did Coach Gluant himself tell you this?"

"He did."

"When did he tell you?"

"When we were making love, Inspector."

Clouseau flashed a suave smile. "Ah, but you toy with me, my dear. You and I, we have not made the love . . . yet."

"Not you! I mean him and me."

"You . . . and Ponton?" Clouseau turned indignantly to his partner. "Ponton, how could you keep this from me? How long have you known this young woman!"

Cherie wedged herself between them. "Not him, you fool!"

Clouseau raised his brow. "I must respectfully request that you do not call my associate a fool. He may not be the sharpest stick in the crayon box, but—"

Cherie leaned in until her nose was almost touching Clouseau's. "Read my lips, Inspector—I was *sleeping* with Yves."

"Who is this woman, this mysterious . . . Eve?"

"Yves Gluant! *Yves Gluant!*"

Clouseau eyed her shrewdly. "I must ask you not to leave town, mademoiselle. You display a temper most formidable. You will make a charming addition to Clouseau's list of the suspect."

Her eyes flashed, her nostrils flared. "You *boob!*"

Clouseau touched Ponton's sleeve. "Please. He is new."

With an exasperated sigh, the young woman pointed to a man in dark sweats who had just entered the gymnasium.

"*That's* who you want to talk to!" she said, and folded her arms.

Rugged, with curly hair and a rather pointed chin, the new arrival seemed less than friendly as he approached.

"I understand you wish to see me," he said.

"This depends," Clouseau said.

"On what?"

"On who you are."

"My name is Vainqueur—and I'm in charge around here. Who the hell are you?"

Clouseau exchanged pointed glances with Ponton, then said, "I am Inspector Jacques Clouseau. You have perhaps heard of me?"

"No."

Ponton began to write that down, and Clouseau stopped him.

"What do you want?" Vainqueur snapped. "We're busy here. Training is a year-round affair for Team France."

Raising an eyebrow, Clouseau said, "I understand there are *many* . . . 'affairs' in these circles."

Vainqueur gave Cherie a suspicious look. Then the new head coach said, "I told you I am a busy man."

"As am I," Clouseau said. "As am I."

"Then *get* busy!"

Clouseau arched another eyebrow, his lips pursing. "I am told that around here . . . *many* people 'get busy' . . ."

"Listen, you pompous little ass." Vainqueur got in Clouseau's face. "If you have any questions, spit them out! I am in no mood for innuendo."

"Then we will chase to the cut—how did you feel about Coach Gluant? Do you in fact . . . *hate* him? Or perhaps . . . *despise* him? Or might I say . . . *abhor* him?"

Vainqueur backed off. "And what if I did?"

"I would have to point out that he has been killed."

A short snort and a shrug came from the new coach. "Not every death is a tragedy."

"No, monsieur . . . but every murder is a crime! Why did you hate this man?"

The reply was almost a snarl. "Wouldn't *you* hate someone who kept you under his thumb, and verbally abused you every day?"

Ponton was nodding.

The new coach continued: "Six years I spent at the whim of this egomaniac—I was no fan of Yves Gluant."

Eyes tight, Clouseau said, "And yet now you have this murdered man's job . . . ironic, is it not?"

"I do not see the irony, Inspector. Are we finished here?"

Ponton whispered to Clouseau, "I don't see the irony, either, Inspector."

Clouseau said, "Listen! Learn! Take your notes and do not—"

Through a nearby doorway came distant footsteps. Echoing. Echoing . . .

"*This* is your opportunity, my simple colleague! You will observe firsthand the skills of Jacques Clouseau . . ."

"Inspector," Vainqueur said, "I have—"

"Shush!"

Clouseau listened to the sounds carefully, and then, in a soft yet sharp voice translated them: "High heels, these footsteps. Rather formal ones for this time of day, I would say . . . five feet two. Brunette. I would say . . . thirty to thirty-five years old, *n'es-ce pas*?"

A rather unprepossessing man in sweats entered, hauling soccer balls and a training bag.

Clouseau reared back. "Is anyone with you?"

"What?" the man said.

Clouseau leaned into the hallway. No one was around.

"Where is she?" he demanded of the stubby man.

"Where is who?"

"You were with no one?"

"No. No one."

The inspector's eyes narrowed with their characteristic shrewdness. "Are you perhaps wearing *pumps*?"

"What? Are you mad? No!" He pointed to tennis shoe-shod feet.

Desperate, Clouseau asked, "How tall are you?"

"I am five foot six."

Clouseau whirled in triumph to his small audience. "Ah ha! Did I not *say* five foot six?"

"Actually," Cherie said, "you said five foot two. But he is rather short, I will grant you."

To Ponton the inspector said, "Listen. Learn."

The man in sweats blurted, "Who are you, anyway? What is this about?"

Clouseau drew in a deep breath. "I?" He exhaled grandly. "I am Inspector Clouseau. And this? . . . This is about . . . *murder!*"

The word echoed through the gym, and Clouseau glanced all around in self-satisfaction. No one, however, had reacted—soccer practice and workouts continued unabated; neither did Cherie, Vainqueur, the little man in sweats, or even Ponton show any response.

These ones, they play their cards close to the vest, Clouseau thought.

Clouseau planted himself before their latest arrival, the small man in sweats. "And you are?"

"Yuri. I am the trainer."

"I see. I see. And what is it that you do here?"

"Well . . . train."

Clouseau grunted a derisive laugh. "And what would the Team France have need for, with the locomotive engineer? It is absurd!"

Ponton leaned forward. "He trains the athletes."

"I know that! What are you writing down, there?"

"Nothing, Inspector . . . Nothing."

Clouseau resumed his inquiry. "Monsieur Yuri . . . the trainer who trains . . . did you know Coach Gluant?"

Yuri shrugged. "Of course. We all knew him. He was the coach."

"Ah. And how did he come to hire you?"

"Well, he sought me out. He and Cherie. I was with the Russian team; I had a good reputation, and he stole me away."

"Stole you away! And how did he manage this, this theft?"

"He paid me more than the Russians."

"The higher-pay ploy. Did you like Gluant?" Clouseau thrust himself forward. "Or did you perhaps . . . *hate* him?"

"As a matter of fact," Yuri said, "I liked and admired him very much."

"And how do I know this is not the deceptive lie? . . . *You are not to leave France!*"

Yuri looked distraught. "But our next game is not *in* France, Inspector."

"You are not to leave Europe!"

"Our next games are in Asia . . ."

"Asia? Well . . . Asia is all right. *But you are not to leave Asia or Europe!*"

Vainqueur piped in. "We do have a game coming up in Brazil."

Clouseau turned to the coach and considered his words, saying, "I see. Brazil." Then he whirled back to the trainer. "But you are not to leave Europe! Or Asia! Or . . . or the Americas!"

Yuri shrugged, said, "No problem," and went off with the tools of his trade.

Clouseau returned his attention to the somewhat hostile head coach. "Monsieur Vainqueur—this fellow Bizu. Would you say he hated Gluant?"

"Most definitely."

"Enough to . . . *kill* him?"

"That would be your job to find out, isn't it?"

"Do you know where he is now?"

"Yes."

Clouseau nodded. Swallowed. "Might you share that information with us?"

"Well, he's outside. On the practice field."

"And what would he be doing there?"

". . . Practicing."

"Yes. Yes. I know something of this, the need of practice for the skilled athlete."

The coach smiled a little. "Do tell."

"Yes." Clouseau made a modest shrug, and displayed a small example of a karate chop in the air. "You see, I have the black belt."

"I'm sure it holds your trousers up nicely. Cherie will show you the way . . . If you'll excuse me, Inspector? Some of us have *real* work to do."

Clouseau watched the man cross the gym floor to hook up with several of the team members at a practice net, where he began to give instructions.

To Ponton, Clouseau said, "Do you detect a hint of attitude there, my sizeable comrade?"

"Yes, Inspector. He is an asshole."

"Ah. Ah, is *that* what it is? Very keenly observant on your part, Ponton. You stay here and ask any follow-up questions of our suspects that might occur to you. Clouseau will take on the great Bizu, as the Italians say, 'mano a mano' . . ."

"I believe that's the Spanish, Inspector," Ponton said.

"Well, it may be the Spanish as well . . ."

"Or maybe the Mexicans . . ."

"Ponton! You have your orders. Carry them out."

"Yes, Inspector."

Clouseau did not immediately begin his interview with Bizu. He had found in his numerous years of investigatory work that studying a sus-

pect in advance—from a distance, before revealing himself as a detective—could reveal much
about the character of said suspect. So he took a
place high in the stands, by himself, and watched
his prey.

This was not a great stadium, just a practice
field, and the stands were like those at the small
high school in Fromage. This meant that
Clouseau was above Bizu, but close enough that,
eventually, eye contact could be made . . .

His black hair like a nest of snakes, the darkly
handsome soccer star had the field to himself,
kicking balls. His strokes were expert, but anger
lurked within each kick, as if every rubber orb
were the head of an enemy.

Considering this, his steel-trap mind process-
ing his observations, Clouseau—idly fiddling
with a small screw attached to the back of the
bench—finally decided the time had come to call
himself to the attention of the star player.

After much thought about what he might say,
what precise remark might put Bizu off his guard
and let his adversary know that he was dealing
with a mastermind detective with whom he dare
not trifle, Clouseau called out, "Nice kick!"

Then the inspector sat back and smiled, with
just a hint of sneer, almost unconsciously playing
with that little screw to combat the small touch of
nervousness that even a brave officer like
Clouseau—being after all human—possessed.

Bizu turned and glared up at the lone figure at the top of the stands.

Their eyes locked.

The tension between them was telling, indeed—Clouseau almost could hear the gears turning; it was as if Bizu's very thought processes had begun to creak. Clouseau saw the star weaving out there, his footing unsure, the poor fool thrown off by the deadly gaze of Clouseau.

"What are *you* looking at?" Bizu called.

Ah, Clouseau thought; *the battle of the wits— the war of the nerves . . .*

"I am looking at *you*, my friend. The prime suspect in the murder of Yves Gluant!"

"Am I really?" the star yelled. "And what are you going to do about it?"

"I? I am going to—"

And the bleachers gave way—it had been the stands that had been swaying, not Bizu, the structure itself that had been creaking, not the star's thoughts—and they folded dramatically, like venetian blinds, sending the great detective sliding down . . .

Fortunately, this improvised passage was as smooth and unbroken as a ski slope. And the only thing that gave Clouseau away, just a bit, was his scream as he came gliding down.

But he regained his composure by landing, like a cat, on his feet—*better* than a cat, because he required only two feet—as if he had planned this dramatic entrance, all along.

Ever so suavely he said to the soccer star, whose face was only a few inches away from the inspector's own, ". . . I am going to invite you to join me."

Flecks of sweat flew as Bizu demanded, "For what? Where?"

"To the headquarters."

Bizu shook his head, more sweat flicking onto Clouseau, who blinked it away. "Do you mind I dress?"

"In fact I would prefer it," Clouseau said with great dignity. "The nudity publique, she is a crime, also . . . though not as serious as . . . *murder!*"

"I will keep that in mind," Bizu said with a smirk.

But he complied.

In an interrogation chamber in the bowels of the Palais de la Justice, a spotlight was on the star player; but not the kind of spotlight he was accustomed to: this was the bright hot light of what the Americans called the Third Degree. Shadows fell dramatically in the closet of a room, stripes of black, bars of white, as if Bizu already were in prison.

Bizu sat on a bare wooden chair; nearby was a

small table, and another chair. But the inspector stood, rocking on his heels, appraising his interviewee with harsh eyes.

Then, suddenly, Clouseau thrust himself into the man's face and yelled, *"You are the soccer player known as Bizu?"*

Bizu seemed more confused than frightened. "Yes."

"And you were acquainted with Yves Gluant?"

"Yes. Of course. He was my coach. Everyone knows that."

"Do not tell Clouseau what he knows! Only Clouseau knows what he knows! . . . How did you feel about this coach?"

Bizu grunted. "I hope he's burning in hell at this very moment."

"Ah!" Clouseau ratcheted up the volume further. *"Then it is true that you disliked him?"*

A smirk crinkled the upper lip of the suspect. "Let's just say I'm not crying over him pushing up daisies."

"He is not pushing up the daisies! He is dead! What do the daisies have to do—"

"It's an expression—idiom."

Clouseau reared back, fury in his eyes. *"You— you sir, are the idiom!"*

Bizu rolled his eyes.

Then the inspector was on him again, speaking quickly, voice dripping with menace, rife with threat: *"Unless you wish to spend the rest of your nat-*

ural life in prison, where much is unnatural, particularly in the showers, you will answer my next question . . . Did . . . you . . . kill . . . Gluant?"

Bizu lurched forward on the chair, until he and Clouseau were touching noses. "I only wish that I had! How I would have loved it! Only someone . . . some lucky bastard . . . beat me to it!"

Clouseau drew back. He looked at the suspect with contempt. "You . . . you disgust me."

Bizu hung his head.

"One moment," Clouseau said, his voice softer, "we will continue this."

Bizu said nothing, staring at the floor.

Clouseau stepped out.

Moments later he returned; his expression was wholly different—pleasant, as was his soft-spoken tone as he asked, "Would you like a cigarette, my friend?"

Bizu blinked in surprise. "Uh, no. No thanks. I'm an athlete. I don't smoke."

"Good! This is a very good decision. This is why we are so proud of our athletes here in France." He moved closer, leaned down and beamed at the suspect. "Bizu, my friend, I just wanted you to know that I know you didn't do this crime."

"What? . . . Oh. Well. Good. That's nice."

Clouseau pulled up the spare chair. "Someone else did this terrible thing . . . and now they are doing another terrible thing: putting you in the picture frame with the gilt around it."

Bizu swallowed, sat forward. "You may be right . . . Can you help me, Inspector?"

"It would be my pleasure. My honor." He shifted on the chair. "Tell me, my friend—do *you* have any idea who might have done this thing?"

Bizu laughed bitterly. "Where to start? This list is long. But you've been looking at the team, haven't you? I would suggest Gluant's business interests."

The inspector's eyes narrowed. "Ah. And what interests are these?"

"He had money in some stupid chain of restaurants. His partner was that fellow Larocque . . . the casino owner?"

"Raymond Larocque?"

"The very man, Inspector. You see, Gluant would steal money from the restaurants to feed his gambling habit. But Gluant was such an arrogant bastard that he would *brag* about it! I'm not the only one he told about Larocque, and what a sucker he considered the man to be."

"And you suspect Larocque?"

"You have lots of prime candidates, Inspector. But that's my best guess, yes—that Larocque got fed up with Yves and had him killed. The Pink Panther stone would've gone a long way to make up what Gluant stole, and beyond. And this casino owner has the mob connections to make it happen, too."

Clouseau's eyes flashed. "Ah! The mob. The syndicate. The Mafia. It was inevitable, was it not, that they would rear their filthy heads?"

Bizu's upper lip again curled bitterly. "All I know is that whoever did this did the world a favor. Gluant was a selfish, conceited, stinking pig!"

Clouseau cast a smile upon his suspect and patted him on the shoulder. "I like you, Bizu. You have the good heart . . . If you'll excuse me?"

The inspector entered the small adjacent chamber where Ponton had been watching through the two-way glass.

"You're doing fine, Inspector," the big man said. "You've pulled a lot of good information out of Bizu. But what exactly is this technique you're using?"

Clouseau removed from a desk drawer a small black electrical box with a small plunger at its center top, not unlike an explosives detonator.

"My inexperienced friend! Are you not familiar with the classic good-cop-bad-cop ploy?"

Ponton looked momentarily stunned, like a clubbed baby seal. "But . . . don't usually *two* different cops do that . . . ?"

Clouseau shrugged. "Well, that is an option, I suppose. But my approach, she is more efficient, what with budgets and so on . . . Watch and learn, my ample assistant . . ."

Clouseau entered the interrogation booth, ominously brandishing the small electrical box. His entire manner had changed; he projected a sinister, sadistic side. Again he all but shouted at the suspect.

"*And, so, Bizu . . . you may have heard what we do to the suspect who does not cooperate.*"

Bizu, confused, insisted, "But, Inspector—I *did* cooperate!"

"*Do not contradict me! . . . If you do not continue to cooperate, I will have to hook you up to . . . the box.*"

Bizu swallowed thickly, genuinely afraid. "And what . . . what is 'the box'?"

"*Simply these two electrodes,*" Clouseau said, pointing them out. "*Attached to the suspect's . . . testicles!*"

Bizu paled.

"*One,*" Clouseau said nastily, "*each . . .*"

Apparently interested, Bizu leaned forward. "How exactly does it work, Inspector?"

"*It is child's play, you idiom!*" His voice heavy with threat, Clouseau said, "*It is like this . . . one goes here, the other goes there . . .*"

Demonstrating, he dropped his pants and attached the electrodes to the desired points of potential pain.

"And, please, my friend," Clouseau said softly, reverting to the good cop, seeing Bizu's hand reaching out toward the plunger, "do *not* touch that . . ."

The scream emerging from the interrogation room rang and echoed throughout the bowels and up into the halls of the Palais de la Justice, where many a seasoned police officer shuddered, wondering what poor miscreant was getting "the box" today.

SEVEN

A Suspect Eliminated

Chief Inspector Charles Dreyfus was by defini-
tion a newsmaker, but he—like so many public
figures—was also a captive of the news. And as
he and his deputy watched the evening news on
a television in the chief inspector's office, Dreyfus
felt that emotion, of all emotions, that so dis-
tressed a powerful man: helplessness.

The coverage of Clouseau at the press conference had, on the surface, gone exactly as Dreyfus
had planned—the bumbling inspector had been
put at the center of the public's perception of the
case, providing the perfect distraction while the
real genius detective—Dreyfus himself—went

about his investigation unimpeded, supplanted by the Police Nationale's best investigators.

But this . . . this was exceeding his expectations, and not necessarily in a positive way.

The smooth male news anchor was saying, "*And then the inspector, pulled from the ranks of obscure hinterlands service into the forefront of this important investigation, boldly sent a personal message to the murderer.*"

A close-up of Clouseau—speaking directly to the camera, and hence staring with those dangerously eager eyes right at the chief inspector—consumed the monitor screen.

"*To* you *killer, I say*—I will find you!"

Dreyfus touched his left eye where it had begun, just a little, to twitch; he stroked the area gently, thinking, *I could really use a message.* Then he winced and blurted, "Massage! *Massage!*"

Renard looked over with concern at his superior, seated behind the grand desk. "Are you all right, Chief Inspector?"

"Yes . . . yes . . ."

On the screen Clouseau was saying, "*Because I am a servant of our great nation . . . because justice is justice . . . and because France . . . is* France!"

"Gibberish," Dreyfus murmured. "Sheer gibberish."

The anchor was on screen, saying, "*The media has already found a designation for this new superstar sleuth—the Pink Panther Detective.*"

Dreyfus groaned.

"It is rare in this modern world," the anchor continued, *"for a hero to emerge, a new hero to bring hope to a nation still mourning the loss of its legendary coach, Yves Gluant."*

"Shut it off," Dreyfus said, shuddering. "Shut the thing off."

"Yes, sir," Renard said, and did.

"The Pink Panther Detective! Why not the Green Jackass Imbecile!"

"Unlikely to catch on with the public, sir."

Dreyfus shot his second-in-command a reproving glance. "Your humor is not appreciated, Renard. We may have a problem."

"Aren't things going to plan, Chief Inspector? The reports from our investigators began to come in, and—"

Dreyfus rose from his desk and began to pace. "With no findings of note whatsoever! And in the meantime, while our people diligently work to little reward, this absurdity with a mustache has done absolutely nothing, and already he is portrayed by the press as a national hero!"

Renard shrugged. "He did give them a good sound bite."

"There is nothing 'sound' about Jacques Clouseau, Renard. He is a moron of the first rank. At times I wonder if anyone could really be as stupid as he . . ."

Abruptly, Dreyfus's pacing halted.

Spinning toward his deputy, the chief inspector had a wild look in his eyes.

"Renard—is it possible . . . that he may not be as stupid as we think . . . ?"

Renard's eyebrows lifted. "It seems difficult to conceive that any human being could be *that* stupid."

"Yes! Yes!" He thrust a finger at his assistant. "We must be very careful, Renard—we must be careful of this seeming fool. Perhaps he is not the bumbler we take him for. Perhaps it is all a clever ruse!"

Considering that, Renard said, "If so, Chief Inspector—it is a *thorough* ruse, indeed . . ."

As they strode down the marble steps of the elegant Palais de la Justice, Clouseau and Ponton discussed the Pink Panther case.

The inspector was pleased with the results of his interrogation of the soccer star, Bizu.

"Ponton," he was saying, "this man may be the athlete of the great abilities, he may have the fitness physical, but he cannot stand up under the advanced interrogation techniques of Inspector Jacques Clouseau!"

And indeed, only minor wisps of smoke were emerging from his trousers now, following his use of the electrical box.

"Have you come to a conclusion about Bizu, Inspector?" the towering assistant asked, as they approached the Renault, where Clouseau had parked it, backward.

"I have! . . . Have you?"

With a decisive gesture of the forefinger, Ponton said, "I think he is our best suspect. I would say that this Bizu is very likely the guilty party."

The inspector laughed lightly, as if feeling sorry for his charge. "Ah, my inexperienced if oversized waif . . . Allow Papa Clouseau to explain."

Soon they were in the Renault, which was a bit of a squeeze for Ponton, who nonetheless (at Clouseau's bidding) got behind the wheel. Clouseau elucidated, as they drove through the scenic streets of Paris.

"*Fact*—Gluant suspended Bizu."

Ponton nodded.

"*Fact*—Gluant stole from Bizu the affections of the lovely Xania, certainly a woman of considerable charms, easily worth killing over."

Again Ponton nodded.

"*Fact*—from the most important game of the year, Gluant removes Bizu and consigns him in shame to the bench."

Ponton nodded once more.

"*Fact*—Bizu had the perfect opportunity to commit the crime, in the chaos that followed the team's great victory."

Ponton said, "So, then, you agree—Bizu is guilty."

Clouseau's eyes flared. "Don't be absurd! He is clearly *not* guilty! He is innocent."

"But Inspector . . . working from all these facts, how do you come to this conclusion?"

"Instinct!"

Stunned by this, Ponton double-parked in front of Clouseau's apartment building and said, "Inspector, if Gluant had done these things to me, I would have done *exactly* what Bizu did. I would have gladly killed him!"

Clouseau eyed his partner. "And where were you on the afternoon of the murder?"

"You can't be serious!"

"Ponton, my large friend with the moderate mind, I am always serious. Remember at all times, Ponton—there is nothing funny about crime."

And the inspector flung open the car door, by way of emphasis, knocking a passing bicyclist flying off his bike, windmilling through the air.

Not noticing this, Clouseau continued his lesson as he emerged into the street from the Renault. "Ponton, a mystery is like the jigsaw puzzle. Having the jig alone is not enough—one must also have . . . the saw."

Just up the block, the bicyclist, sitting up on the cement, began to groan.

"Did you say something, Ponton? . . . No? My friend, you must at all times be observant. Because murder, she takes no holiday. And your mind must be like the Swiss watch, precise and full of gears and little wheels, turning, turning."

Turning, Clouseau promptly tripped over the bicycle that lay where its owner had left it.

"This, this, this, for example!" Clouseau said, jumping to his feet, gesturing to the bike, a wheel spinning. "This abandoned bicycle—it could be the clue of some crime. Did it come from the sky? I think not. Somewhere, there is a story about this abandoned bike—was it stolen? Did some fiend cause harm to its owner?"

"*God*-damn-*it!*"

"What did you say, Ponton?"

"Nothing," Ponton said. "Sounds like someone may have been hurt down the street . . ."

Clouseau smiled bitterly. "Ah, the city. There are millions of stories in the city which is naked; this you will learn, my friend—park the car, would you, Ponton, and join me in my flat? We should go over what we have discovered on our first day on the job."

Down the street, the bicylist had made it to his feet and was glaring red-faced at the oblivious Clouseau.

"*Bastard!*" the biker screamed, waving fists.

Clouseau looked behind him, to see who this excited devil was calling out to.

Charging toward Clouseau like an enraged bull, the biker barreled through the intersection just as a large globe of the world came rolling down the incline of the adjacent street, traveling at enormous speed, knocking over the poor fellow in its wake, taking him with it.

Ponton, from the doubled-parked car, bent down to look across through the passenger window at Clouseau and asked, "What do you make of that, Inspector?"

Clouseau swallowed, shrugged, and said, "The world, how she turns, it is a mystery even the greatest detective can never hope to solve . . . Park the car, Ponton. And check in with the headquarters! See if there have been the developments."

"Yes, Inspector."

Clouseau was right: murder took no holiday, not on the Pink Panther case, at least.

At the very moment he and Ponton were discussing the guilt or innocence of Bizu, the great soccer player himself was getting out of his exercise gear in the Team France locker room.

Hearing footsteps, he looked up.

Bizu saw a familiar face and, in his usual brusque way, said, "Oh it's you—what do you want?"

The reply was unusual to say the least—exemplified by the red light of a laser on the star's forehead, as a weapon was sighted.

The reflexes of Bizu were second to none among the great athletes of Europe. But when the bullet pierced his forehead, those reflexes were instantly shut down, and he dropped to the floor, a well-trained machine that would never run again.

The gunshot as well as the sound of the body falling to the floor—for indeed it was a body, a corpse, no longer a man—was heard only by one party. The lovely PR rep of Team France, Cherie Dubois, had been passing by.

Tentatively, she stuck her head into the locker room; normally, as a woman, she respected the privacy of these male athletes—not that some of them wouldn't have relished the opportunity to strut around in front of her. Still, it was too late in the day for anyone to be in the locker room at all . . .

So she merely called in: "What was *that?* . . . Is everything all right? Everyone all—"

But the question choked off, when she saw the trickle of red making its way across the cement floor toward her.

Opening the door wider, she saw Bizu, sprawled near the bench, and she screamed.

The great player had gone out the last way he ever would have wanted to: once and for all, benched.

As he approached his apartment door, Inspector Clouseau reached a hand into his pants pocket for his keys; but he paused.

There would be no need for a key.

His door was already ajar . . .

Like Bizu, Clouseau had finely honed instincts. And from under his arm came the revolver that had been presented to him by his chief in Fromage. Many detectives used automatic handguns these days, nine millimeter weapons a strong preference in the profession; but not Clouseau. He favored the old-fashioned joys of a revolver— there was no danger of jamming. Such a weapon was entirely reliable.

But he did not remember if he had loaded it, prior to leaving Fromage, and so—ever the master of detail—he broke open the well-oiled weapon to make sure. It was indeed ready for action: six bullets nestled in their little metal berths. Clouseau grinned confidently to himself, pitying the intruder who had risked incurring his wrath. He snapped the chamber back in place.

The weapon was, perhaps, too well-oiled, as the cylinder bounced back open. When Clouseau—in proper procedure—raised the weapon, snout up, the bullets fell like brittle rain to the hallway floor, the weapon emptying itself.

Clouseau whirled at the sound, saw nothing.

Unaware that his weapon was empty, he stepped close to the door—it was not open wide enough for him to get any kind of view within the flat—and his trained police officer's mind kicked into gear.

Thinking, *I must check for the trap for the booby*, he stepped high on tiptoes to run a finger along the doorsill's top.

As he was doing this, Nicole—within Clouseau's apartment—was in the process of doing some laundry for the man she'd been assigned to help. Walking from the kitchen carrying two freshly laundered shirts of the inspector's, she noted the door standing ajar, and gave it a helpful kick.

Hanging by a wedged finger from the closed door, Clouseau was able through his phenomenal strength of will, to suppress a scream, merely thrashing in pain and weeping silently. Swinging back and forth, he did his best to reach the doorbell, but could not.

Luckily, the inspector always had other options. It was unorthodox, he knew, but he would fire a bullet into the bell and ring it thusly. And so he learned that his weapon was empty.

Composing himself, methodically going through the file cards of his mind to discern the most dignified response to this crisis, Clouseau—hanging by an ever reddening digit—began to kick wildly at the door.

Nicole, in the kitchen, heard the racket and answered it.

Clouseau fell in a pile of flesh, bones, clothing and humiliation at her feet.

"I humble myself before you, my dear," he said, looking up at the lovely girl.

"Oh, Inspector! Your finger!"

"Yes . . . this . . . this is my finger . . ."

"What have I done?"

He allowed himself to be helped to his feet. "You have done the impossible, my dear. You have shown the fraility of the man you assume to be perfection. You have revealed the frightened little boy behind the mask of the great detective."

"Oh, Inspector . . . come in . . . It must be throbbing! May I rub something on that?"

"Certainly . . . but first—my finger."

In the kitchen, Clouseau sat at the table while the chief inspector's secretary applied salve to a finger swollen to the size of a summer sausage.

"Oh dear . . . oh dear. It's so large, Inspector."

"Thank you. But why are you here, in my private sanctuary, my sweet little salve-applying swan?"

Pretty eyelashes batted behind the glasses. "I let myself in with a key . . . I hoped you wouldn't mind."

She explained that his two new suits had come back from the tailor. Then as she was getting him a bottle of water from the refrigerator, she noticed a hardboiled egg in a bowl; very little else was in there. She took the liberty of removing the egg and, as she handed him a bottle of water, asked, "May I have this? It's been a terribly long day, Inspector, and I haven't had a bite since lunch."

"If you need a bite, my dear, you have come to

the right place. Indulge yourself. Indulge. What is mine is yours!"

She removed the shell at the sink, Clouseau at the table, his back to her. Holding the egg before her as if it were a precious jewel, perhaps the Panther itself, she suddenly felt how slippery the thing was, and before she knew it, the egg had squirted from her fingertips into her mouth, lodging there.

Unable to speak or breathe, she gyrated helplessly behind the seated inspector.

Who was expounding upon his philosophy of investigation. "You see, Nicole, for the great detective, it is necessary to be aware of everything that happens around him at all times. And this investigation, she is demanding like the small child with the hunger."

Nicole's hands flapped at her chest, her face turning a bright shade of red.

"If we are not observant," Clouseau was saying, "we are unable to rise to the occasion. In this case, the case of the Pink Panther, I find it is necessary for me to bring into play everything I have learned in a lifetime of investigation. Things begin to appear in the mind that I do not remember ever having known. Have you ever heard of anything so strange, my pet?"

"*Urrrrk,*" Nicole said. "*Urrrk.*"

Puzzled, as her response seemed to be in a tongue other than the many he had mastered,

Clouseau turned to Nicole, and saw her with the white end of the egg projecting from her lips, her eyes huge, whites showing all around, her color a deep lush purple.

"Mon dieu!" Clouseau said, on his feet now. "Le Heimlich! Le Heimlich!"

He flew to her, swivelled her around, his arms encircling her waist from behind, lifting her high off the ground.

"Ahhh!" Clouseau blurted. "Yes! Yes! Ahhh! *Ahhhh!*"

He did not hear the knock at his apartment door, and soon Ponton had entered the kitchen, to see Clouseau lifting Nicole off the floor from behind, thrusting wildly.

It seemed to Ponton that the Police Nationale's one-woman welcome wagon was outdoing herself where the inspector was concerned.

Clouseau, in the midst of the Heimlich manuever, glanced back at Ponton and said, "Don't worry, Ponton! We have almost made it!"

The egg shot from Nicole's lips and flew out the nearest window.

"Ahhhhhh," she said, as he lowered her to the floor.

"Do you feel better, my dear?" the inspector asked, a hand on her shoulder as she bent, hands on knees, breathing hard.

Ponton watched, amazed.

She worked at getting back her breath. "Nothing . . . nothing like that has ever happened to me before . . ."

"Well," Clouseau said, flashing Ponton a smile, "it was lucky I was here, then—you could not have done that alone!"

Nicole said, "Yes, yes, *merci*, Inspector, *merci*. You are so good at that! Where did you learn it?"

"Well, in Fromage, we practice on the manikins."

Ponton's eyes narrowed. "Really?"

Clouseau nodded. "Ponton, remember, it is best done from behind. And Nicole, well—she really needed it!"

"Ah," Ponton said.

Clouseau gestured to the kitchen table and all three sat.

"Ponton, did you check with the headquarters?"

"I did."

"And what have you learned?"

Ponton shook his head. "What I learned, Inspector, what I continue to learn . . . is not to doubt you, and your . . . unusual abilities."

"Good! Good! . . . Why?"

"Well—you seem to have been right about our friend Bizu. He was just found in the training facility locker room—shot in the head . . . right here."

Ponton tapped his forehead.

Clouseau's eyes narrowed in their characteristically shrewd manner. "I see. And who does Bizu say did this thing to him?"

"Uh . . . he was shot in the head, Inspector."

"Ah yes. Was it fatal?"

"Well—yes."

"How fatal?"

"I would say—completely fatal."

Clouseau pondered. "Then speaking to him would be . . . out of the question."

"Well, he *is* dead."

"Were there witnesses?"

"Only one—Cherie Dubois."

Clouseau nodded. "The beauty with the temper. Our witness is also . . . a suspect!" He looked at Nicole firmly. "My ample assistant and I must go. While I am gone, Nicole—put nothing in your mouth!"

Nicole said, "Not until you return, Inspector."

Now Ponton was doing the pondering, as the pair of detectives departed.

Within the hour, Clouseau and Ponton were in the locker room at the Team France facility. The body had not been removed, a chalk outline drawn around it. The attractive blonde PR rep stood as far away from the corpse as possible while still remaining in the room. A gendarme was beside her.

Clouseau bent over the body. "Ponton . . . take a look at this . . . Strange . . . most strange . . ."

The big man crouched on the opposite side of Bizu's body.

With keen eyes on his partner, Clouseau said, "Do you not think this is the coincidence odd?"

"What is, Inspector?"

"That this man, he should be shot and fall precisely, perfectly within this outline on the floor?"

"Uh . . . Inspector, I believe that was done later."

Clouseau's eyes flashed. "Are we dealing with a madman? Who would kill a man, and take the chalk and—"

"No, no—here in the city, we mark the position of the body with chalk. So the body can be moved, and we still have an idea of—"

Clouseau jerked to his feet. "I know this! Do not patronize me, Ponton! I was . . . testing you. Well done! I applaud you. And now for this wench with the temper . . ."

The inspector approached the young woman, whose arms were folded as if she were cold—indeed she was shivering . . . with fear.

"Mademoiselle Dubois, please—tell me precisely what you saw. Leave *nothing* out!"

She gulped and nodded and said, "I didn't see anything, really. I was passing by the locker room. It was late, past the time that anyone is usually around, but I could hear someone on the other side of the door. Moving around? Then I heard Bizu say something like, 'Oh, it's you.'

Well, I didn't figure this was any of my business, so I started down the hall, when I heard a sound that must have been gunfire!"

Clouseau said, "Thank you, my child. One moment . . ."

He took Ponton aside and said, "Go to the databases and check that name."

Ponton frowned in confusion. "What name, Inspector?"

" 'You,' you fool! I want to interrogate every person in Paris going by the name of 'You.' "

Ponton began to say something, thought better of it, and made a note.

Clouseau began to pace. "My enormous associate, we must face the facts—we are up against the criminal mastermind!" He tripped over the corpse, sprang to his feet, muttering, "Swine victim!"

Ponton leaned forward. "Are you all right, Inspector?"

"I have never been better! For I have made a decision."

"What decision is that, Inspector?"

"This murder . . . these murders . . . for we now have more than one murder, and that is a larger number, *n'est pas*? . . . these murders, they speak of sophistication. And what is more sophisticated, my friend, than a casino?"

Ponton smiled a little. "Ah. You wish to interview the casino owner—Larocque."

"Raymond Larocque! Yes! He alone of our suspects fits the profile of the potential mastermind . . . Which of his casinos is his base of operations, Ponton?"

"The most beautiful city in the world, Inspector."

Clouseau frowned. "I was not aware that gambling was legal in Cleveland."

"Actually, Inspector—I meant Rome."

"Ah." Clouseau shrugged. "To each his own. But in Cleveland there is the Rock and Roll Museum—what is there to see in Rome but a bunch of ruins?"

"And a murderer?" Ponton suggested.

"And a murderer! You are learning. You are learning . . ."

Clouseau returned to Cherie. "My dear—when you discovered the body, what did you do? What did you say?"

"Well, I just sort of . . . stuck my head in, Inspector. It's the men's locker room, after all."

"I understand. You are the shy flower."

"I saw a trickle of red, opened the door wider, and saw Bizu . . . just . . . just . . . *sprawled* on the floor, that terrible wound in his head."

Sagely the inspector nodded. "And what did you do next. What did you say?"

"Well . . . I don't know exactly . . ."

"Think! You must think, cher Cherie. Every detail, it is of vital importance to the investigation criminal!" Clouseau leaned close to the young woman. *"What . . . did . . . you . . . say?"*

"I suppose it was . . ."

And Cherie Dubois screamed in Clouseau's face.

Ears ringing, eyebrows standing up in little exclamation marks, the wide-eyed Clouseau turned to Ponton and said, "Write that down!"

"Yes, Inspector," Ponton said.

Clouseau, after tripping over the corpse again, made his way into the hall.

Cherie approached Ponton and said, "That inspector . . . is he really the perfect fool he seems to be?"

"No one is perfect, mademoiselle," Ponton said, and took his leave.

EIGHT

License to Spill

Outside, where the perpetual premiere of a rotating spotlight's beam cut through the night, the paparazzi and news crews—both local and international—kept a constant vigil for celebrities, a vigil frequently rewarded with flashbulb-worthy prey.

This was, after all, the plushiest casino in Rome, a city fabled for its la dolce vita. Within, smartly dressed men and chicly clothed women, who might well have stepped from the pages of *GQ* and *Vogue*, were attended by young cocktail waitresses with daring decolletage and lovely smiling faces, in a glitteringly appointed gambling den that made Monte Carlo seem shabbily second rate.

Winding among these jet-set patrons, the modestly garbed detectives from France moved like the conspicuous outsiders they were.

Finally, in the midst of the casino, against the familiar din of dealers' voices, gamblers' wagers, spinning balls and flung dice, the trenchcoated Clouseau finally took sudden root, not noticing that he caused a cocktail waitress to lurch into a nearby aisle, spilling her tray of drinks onto several stunned beautiful—and now wet—people.

"Ponton," Clouseau said, "I will mingle. You, my lummox liege, will go to inquire about the office of this Larocque."

"Where will I find you, Inspector?"

"I will be here. Right here. I will . . . blend in."

Ponton was well aware that in their modest police-issue attire, they were brown shoes in this black tux world. But he merely said, "Then you intend to order a drink and gamble?"

"Of course not!" Clouseau shook his head in weary disappointment with his pupil. "First, I am on the duty. An officer does not drink on the duty. Second, neither does he gamble with the wagering. Third, we are servants of the public, on the modest salary—one should only wager when he can afford to lose."

"But you said were going to blend in—"

Clouseau raised a palm. "I will observe from the lines of the side. There is only so much 'blending in' Clouseau can do among such fools."

"Fools?"

"Fools! Look at them, throwing away the money. Do these fools not know that the odds, they are stacked against them? The house, she holds all the cards!"

Ponton, mildly surprised by such relative wisdom coming from the inspector, strode off to fulfill his assignment.

Clouseau watched until his partner was out of sight, then scurried to the nearest roulette table. After much tortured thought, he purchased a single chip, worth a single Euro. Then he placed his bet and his heart pounded.

His eyes followed the little ball as it traveled around and around and around, then stopped.

His jaw dropped.

He had lost.

For some time he stood in stony silence, holding back the tears as he thought of all the things that that Euro could have bought for him.

From his loser's reverie he was shaken when the individual next to him—a suave, dark-haired, wickedly handsome man in evening dress—spoke up loudly in English: *"Such very pleasant weather we're having. I certainly hope this blissful weather continues . . ."*

The words were not intended for Clouseau, rather for a small, somewhat overweight fellow who happened to be standing next to the commanding, dark-haired figure.

"Uh, yes," the confused fellow said. "Isn't it?"

The tall, dark-haired gentleman shrugged slightly to himself, and returned his attention to the roulette table.

But Clouseau leaned in and whispered in English: "I, too, am in the enforcement of the leau."

The tall gentleman frowned in mild confusion. "What do you have to do with the loo?"

"The leau!" Then hushed, Clouseau explained, "The leau enforcement. The force of the police."

"Ah!" Then, after a moment of thought, the tall man said, "Bloody hell . . . was I *that* obvious?"

"No, no, no, monsieur. It is just that I have the nose for words. The ear for spotting my own breed."

A pretty waitress approached and gazed at Clouseau's handsome companion with seemingly real admiration. "Your drink, sir."

"Ah, my mojito. Would you flame it, dear?"

"Certainly, sir."

And, with a flourish, she lit the drink; its flame burned bright, reflecting in Clouseau's wide eyes.

As his new friend took the drink from the waitress and dropped a five-pound note on her tray, Clouseau said, "Impressive. I shall remember that, the flaming-drink ploy. I am Inspector Jacques Clouseau from—"

"France?"

Clouseau smiled. "You are good, monsieur. The details, they do not escape from you." He leaned closer. "I am here to inquire into the theft of the Pink Panther and the murder of our Coach Gluant. A confidential matter that I would not share with just *any* stranger . . ."

"Commendable."

"And you are?"

"Boswell. *Nigel* Boswell. With MI5—agent double oh six. I assume you understand the significance of that?"

"Yes, yes. You are one brick shy of the major load."

Boswell blinked, shrugged that off, then said, "I too am on an important case—very important. And, like you, Inspector—it's confidential."

"You may depend on Inspector Jacques Clouseau, Agent Nigel Boswell!"

Boswell patted the air. "Shhh . . . please, Inspector . . . I am not here."

Clouseau frowned. "Well, of course you are here. Where else would you be?"

"Switzerland."

"Well then, if I were you, I would, how do you British say? Shake the leg. Catch the soonest plane, and—"

"No, no. *Officially* I am there . . . unofficially, I am here."

"Aaahh! Your mission is under the covers."

Boswell twitched a smile. "Frequently, yes . . . Right now I am shadowing a very important

Colombian drug lord. No one must know that I am here."

Clouseau narrowed his eyes. "But if you are under the cover—why do you wear the dress of the evening? This tuxedo is exactly what I would expect of the agent who kills with the license!"

Patiently, Boswell said, "Inspector—*most* men here are wearing tuxedos. In that trenchcoat? You are the exception, not the rule."

Clouseau beamed. "Thank you." Discreetly, seen by no more than a dozen people, Clouseau wrote his cell phone number on a slip of paper. Then he bumped against Boswell, as if accidently.

"Yes," Clouseau said loudly, *"the weather she is blissful . . ."* Then, sotto voce, he said into the agent's ear, "I have just slipped my cell phone number into your pocket . . . *If the clouds, they were any more white* . . . Call me if you need the help of the back."

Spotting Ponton approaching, Clouseau gave the agent a small salute, Boswell nodded almost imperceptibly, and the inspector joined up with his assistant.

"Ponton," Clouseau said, "is our suspect, Larocque, on the premises?"

"He is. We need to check in with security, and—"

As they walked through the crowded casino aisle, Clouseau waved a hand. "Excuse me, I change the subject. Ponton, I must suggest that we suspend our practicing of the attack while we are in the public of the foreign land. We must not attract the attention."

"I agree," Ponton said.

"Splendid. We will resume our training when the circumstances, they are more appropriate."

"That's a good idea, Inspector," Ponton said, and Clouseau tripped him.

The big man was flung down an adjacent aisle. Waitresses and patrons alike tumbled like bowling pins, chips and drinks and ice flying.

"Oh, my friend, you are so clumsy!" Clouseau said, and helped Ponton to his feet. Smiling, Clouseau explained to the spectators, "My friend has the two left foot. He does apologize."

As Clouseau walked him along, Ponton looked at his partner with amazed dismay. "But, Inspector, you said—"

"Vigilance, Ponton! Vigilance . . . and Ponton— trust no one!"

At the casino security desk, Ponton took the lead, saying, "Please inform Monsieur Larocque that Inspector Clouseau of the Police Nationale wishes to have a word with him."

"You are Inspector Clouseau?"

"I am his assistant—Detective Ponton. *This* is Inspector Clouseau . . ."

The security supervisor, an officious but competent-looking individual, gave Clouseau a condescending smirk, and said to Ponton, "You do know that the two of you have no official standing in this country?"

Clouseau stepped forward. "You do not question my authority, in this or any country! We are here with the full knowledge and cooperation of the Interpol!"

The supervisor sighed, nodded and picked up his phone.

Soon, in the elevator, Ponton said, "I was not aware we had coordinated our visit through official channels, Inspector. Did Chief Inspector Dreyfus make the arrangements?"

"Of course not! No such arrangements were made."

Confused, Ponton said, "But you told that security fellow that—"

"He apparently did not know the rule."

"What rule?"

"Have you forgotten so quickly? Trust no one!"

The elevator opened on Larocque's floor, and Ponton tripped Clouseau, who went sprawling onto the carpet.

Jumping to his feet, Clouseau said, "You are the quick learner! I am proud of my pupil. After you, Ponton . . ."

"No, Inspector. I think we will go two abreast, if you don't mind."

Clouseau considered that, and said, "That is an excellent choice, for the breast. Two."

The door to the penthouse suite was answered by a towering, brawny Asian in a Nehru jacket; bald, menacing, frowning, he opened the door without a word.

The two detectives entered to find themselves in a spacious, luxurious penthouse whose modernity was contrasted with an array of elaborately framed impressionist paintings, and Chinese antique furnishings and art pieces. Prominent along one wall was a large, eerily lit fish tank filled with exotic specimen, flashing their fins in seeming greeting.

In the midst of the living room stood a thin, elegant, harshly handsome man in his fifties, vaguely sinister in manner and appearance; his dark suit was cut in the latest European mode, and he leaned on an ornate walking stick of Chinese styling.

Ponton remained in place, at the edge of the living room, while Clouseau—who handed the Asian servant his trenchcoat—confidently wandered the periphery, studying one framed painting after another.

"*Monet!*" he said. Then looking at another, he declared it, "*Renoir!* . . . And this . . . *Gwen-gwan!*"

Their host, with a mild sneer of amusement, said, "Most impressive, Inspector Clouseau. How is it you come to have such knowledge?"

Clouseau said, "I am full of the surprises, my friend. Do not be fooled by my simple country ways. The adversary, he must be kept off the guard, at all times."

With a knowing smile, Clouseau tripped over a coffee table, but leapt to his feet, popping up right before his host. "I am Inspector Jacques Clouseau."

"I know."

"So you have heard of me."

"You called ahead."

"Ah. And you are Raymond Larocque?"

"Yes, I am. And since you feel comfortable revealing your art expertise to me, Inspector, I must say I am highly complimented. You obviously do not regard *me* as an adversary."

"Perhaps, yes. Perhaps, no." Clouseau raised his chin, attempting to look down on the taller man. "I am investigating the murder of Yves Gluant."

Nodding somberly, Larocque said, "Poor Yves —a fascinating, talented man. A genuine loss . . . Would you and your associate like a drink, Inspector?"

From the background, Ponton spoke up. "Thank you, Monsieur Larocque—but we do not drink on duty."

Clouseau said, "Grenadine with a little Pernod."

Larocque's towering Asian servant stepped forward. "This is my majordomo," their host explained. "He's Huang."

To the servant, Clouseau said, "Congratulations. With what organization military did you serve, Major? And what is your name, by the way?"

"That *is* my name, Sweetcheeks," Huang said. He smiled, winked, then scurried off to fill the inspector's drink order.

Clouseau, not knowing what to make of this Sweetcheeks character, switched gears, and again faced his sinister host. "Tell me, Monsieur Larocque—this famous ring the Coach Gluant wore . . . this Pink Panther . . . Do you happen to know how he came to acquire it? Did he *buy* the ring?"

"Oh, no. Certainly not."

The inspector's eyes tensed. "Then he *stole* it?"

A sophisticated smirk appeared on the craggy face. "Well, perhaps that would be the opinion of the maharajahs from the Middle Eastern country where the Panther was first known. Yves inherited it from his grandfather. It cost him nothing."

"Nothing? Nothing but his *life*, monsieur!" Clouseau took a step closer, his eyes locked on those of his host. "May I have a closer look at your bawls?"

Larocque blinked. "Pardon?"

"Your big brass bawls . . . On that table over there? Isn't that large one eighteenth century? Han Dynasty?"

Clouseau thrust a finger toward an ivory table

on which rested beautiful Chinese bowls and vases of varying sizes.

"Be my guest, Inspector. But please—don't touch them."

Clouseau arched an eyebrow. "Really? And why is that?"

"Because some of them are precious."

"Some?"

Larocque shrugged. "Well, you obviously have an eye for antiques. Some are real, some are false."

Clouseau chuckled wisely. "The same can be said of the human being, *nes c'est pas*?"

The inspector approached the ivory table.

His host called, "Inspector—those vases are particularly tricky . . . it's easy to get one's hand caught inside."

Clouseau twirled toward Larocque. "Oh? You do not wish me to look *inside* the vases? Could it be that some worthless copy has something real, something precious within? The Pink Panther, say?"

Larocque scowled. "Don't be ridiculous. Just, please—be careful . . ."

Clouseau picked up a ceramic vase bearing an elaborate Chinese dragon design. "The problem, my friend, is that one must always handle a ceramic vase from the inside—surely you know this! The oil from the hands could change the patina, and effect both the beauty *and* the value . . ."

The inspector, his hand inside the vase now, held it up to the light.

"Ah . . . pure alabaster," he said.

"And nothing else," his host snapped.

"Nothing else . . . *yet*."

Clouseau set his hand-in-vase down on the table, and slipped his hand out—that is, *tried* to slip his hand out . . .

To brace himself, he put a hand on the table—that is, *tried* to put a hand on the table . . .

Instead, he wound up with his left hand in one vase and the right in another.

"That is odd," Clouseau mused. "All I did was follow the acknowledged procedure . . ."

Larocque's teeth were bared. "I *told* you not to put your hand in there, you fool!"

"Is this the way you speak to a guest, sir?!"

Bracing it under his opposite arm, Clouseau attempted to get the first vase off.

As Clouseau did his best to free himself, without damaging the vases, Ponton stepped forward to pick up the interview . . . and cover for his partner.

"Monsieur Larocque," Ponton said, placing his big frame between himself and his struggling associate, "why did you take out a life insurance policy on Yves Gluant?"

"Oh, you know about that, do you?"

"We do."

Larocque shrugged elaborately. "Well, if you

think that makes me a good suspect, I would beg to differ. The insurance company refuses to pay until the murderer is in custody."

From behind Ponton, the struggling, grunting, groaning Clouseau managed, "And what if it is *you* that is in custody, monsieur?"

Larocque snarled, "Then they won't pay me at all, you idiot! . . . When the killer is found, I will get *some* insurance money . . . and I can try to sue the estate against the Pink Panther ring, assuming it's recovered when the killer is captured."

Ponton said, "We do assume that the killer is also the thief."

"Then surely you can see," Larocque said, "that I of all people want the bastard responsible caught!"

Clouseau popped up nearby, his arms behind him (the vases still on his hands). "But, even *aside* from the insurance policy . . . you stood to gain from Gluant's death, did you not?"

"Gain? What in God's name would I gain?"

"Nothing in the name of God," Clouseau said cunningly, his back to the moodily illuminated fish tank. "But in the name of Raymond Larocque? A chain of restaurants! Gluant's share in this chain, she would go to you!"

"The *restaurants*? Don't be ridiculous! That chain was a disaster!"

Pleased with himself, Clouseau leaned back against the tank, inadvertently dipping his elbow into the water. Several exotic fish swam up to greet this intruder—piranha.

Larocque was saying, "Gluant was siphoning money out faster than it was coming in—my only consolation, really, was that he was a degenerate gambler, and would come to my casino and lose that money *back* to me!"

After a brief feeding frenzy, Clouseau drew quickly away from the fish tank, the elbow of his suit shredded and a trifle bloody.

Larocque continued: "But as time went by, Yves's losses exceeded what he'd stolen from me . . . He got into debt with my casino, and, well . . . he promised *me* that ring—as collateral!"

His hands still locked in the vases, his right elbow a ragged mess, Clouseau noted the servant, Huang, entering with the drink on a tray.

Seemingly to Larocque, Clouseau said, "But you had the words angry with Gluant the night before his murder . . ." Spinning toward the servant, Clouseau added, "Did you *not*, Hung-*wang*?"

A vase flew off Clouseau's hand and headed right for the tray with the drink on it; but Huang deftly ducked, and Ponton caught the vase, in a play that marked him the MVP of the interrogation.

"No I *didn't*," Huang pouted.

Clouseau closed in for the kill. "No? You did not threaten to break his arms and his legs and crush them into the little powder?"

"No!"

"Well . . . well . . . well . . ." He shrugged. "I play the hunch."

The inspector turned toward his host. "I believe we have reached the end of the interview . . . By the way, if I may test the skill of your knowledge antique . . ." He hefted the hand still lodged in a vase. ". . . is *this* the copy or an original? Worthless or priceless?"

Larocque shrugged dismissively. "That's an inexpensive copy."

"Ah . . . thank you. That is good." In one of his patented martial arts moves, Clouseau spun toward the ivory table and smashed the vase against it once, twice, three times, finally shattering it . . . and collapsing the ivory table into chunks.

"That table, however," Larocque said, quietly stunned, "is priceless."

Clouseau's mustache twitched. "Not," he said, "anymore . . . Hung-*wang!* My coat, if you please."

As the servant handed him the trenchcoat, the inspector's cell phone rang in a pocket, playing the William Tell Overture, or as Clouseau preferred to think of it, the Lone Ranger theme.

"It is I. Inspector Jacques Clouseau. Speak."

The crisply British voice of the secret agent, Boswell, replied: "It seems I do need back-up, Inspector. Can you meet me in the restaurant, at once?"

"Yes," Clouseau said, climbing into the trench-coat. "Yes, at once!"

"Don't tarry, man. It's urgent!"

"Right away! I will tarry not! The urgency, I understand!"

He clicked off, turned to Larocque, Huang and Ponton and said, "I hope you will excuse me . . . Some, uh, minor matter has come up. Nothing important. Nothing confidential. Nothing having to do with the British Secret Service."

And, leaving shattered antiquities, satisfied fish and confused humans behind him, Clouseau ran from the room.

So diligent was he in his efforts not to tarry, Clouseau—as he passed through the casino—made a small oversight: he failed to notice that masked men in catsuits were robbing it.

He stopped to ask one of these men, who was dressed in skintight black and about to put on a gas mask, directions to the restaurant.

"It is up there," the bandit casually replied in Italian, and pointed to a windowed wall overlooking the casino.

Master of languages that he was, Clouseau automatically understood, replied, "*Merci,*" and headed for the restaurant.

Despite the view onto the casino, the restaurant was dark, the mood intimate, cocktail piano music tinkling. Small private dining areas were spotted here and there, separated off by lush plants and/or half-walls. Barely had Clouseau stepped inside when Nigel Boswell emerged from the shadows of one such intimate corner to take him by the arm to the wall of windows.

"Take a look, Inspector," the secret agent said, "and you will see why I need your assistance . . ."

Out the window Clouseau could see the men in tight black suits wearing gas masks, pulling the pins on gas canisters, plumes of smoke spreading throughout the vast room, the beautiful people turning ugly as they choked.

Boswell pointed and said, "It's as precise as a first-rate military operation."

Indeed, thieves were scooping up money from the tables into laundry bags, while other contingents of masked bandits were at the cashier's booths, helping themselves.

"I would say," Clouseau said shrewdly, "that what we have here is a robbery."

Boswell's eyes flared. "Not just *any* robbery, Inspector—these are the so-called Gas-Mask Bandits . . . all of Europe is after them!"

"Perhaps . . . but it is *we* who are here to *catch* them!" Clouseau struck a martial arts pose. "I am ready and at your secret service."

Boswell held out a hand. "All I need is your coat, really."

"I would give you the shirt off my back!"

"The coat will do nicely."

Clouseau complied. "And how will you deploy me, my friend? What is your plan?"

"My plan is to *be* you, Inspector." Boswell was already getting into the trenchcoat. "I am not supposed to be here—your presence, on the premises, however, is by now well-known."

Clouseau nodded. "It is true—everywhere I go, they know when I have been there."

"So I've noticed." Eyes tight, Boswell lifted a forefinger. "Now it's critical that I *not* blow my cover . . . but at the same time, how can we allow the Gas-Mask Bandits to escape?"

"We cannot."

Buttoned up inside Clouseau's characteristic trenchcoat, Boswell pointed to the floor nearby. "Get my briefcase, would you? There's a good fellow. And put it on the table?"

Clouseau did so, then watched as the agent swiftly unlocked, then snapped open, the briefcase; in holes cut from a black-cushioned bed were an array of the tools of the secret agent trade, among them a gas mask and a laser-beam glass cutter attached to a suction cup. The former Boswell fitted over his face; the latter he used to cut a large square from the window, the suction cup allowing him to merely lift the square out and set it to one side, like a large shield of glass.

Then, using a small pistol-like tool, Boswell shot a steel cord across the casino—it wavered as it went but its trajectory was true.

The inspector watched in open-mouthed admiration as the spy—wearing Clouseau's coat—put on special gloves that aided him in what he did next . . .

. . . which was to slip out the hole in the window to slide across that steel cord, above the casino and the robbery going on below!

And as Boswell made his stunning, sliding, gliding journey using a single gloved hand, he dropped from his free hand a canister that began at once to suck from the air all of the foul gas the bandits had foisted upon the casino and its helpless patrons.

Then that same hand slipped under Clouseau's coat and withdrew another pistol-like weapon.

One by one, Boswell picked off the thieves.

"The sleeping-dart ploy," Clouseau muttered to himself. Those few thieves that Boswell missed on the way across, he snagged on the return journey, for once he got to the opposite wall, he headed back again on his sliding way for the hole in the restaurant's glass wall, beyond which the astounded Clouseau waited.

Landing nimbly before the inspector, Boswell quickly unbuttoned and handed Clouseau back his trenchcoat, into which the inspector slipped. Then he handed Clouseau the gas mask, and dropped the other gizmos into either pocket of the coat.

"Souvenirs?" Clouseau asked. "Thank you, my friend! I will treasure them always—"

"Not souvenirs, Inspector," Boswell said, straightening his black tie, having become once again just another smoothly tuxedoed (if particularly distinguished) casino-goer. "*Evidence* . . . evidence that *you*, not I, are the intrepid bloke who captured the Gas-Mask Bandits."

"I . . . a bloke . . . ?"

Boswell's chin jutted. "You must swallow your pride, Inspector—do me this favor, and take the credit. You will be doing Nigel Boswell and Her Majesty's government a great service."

Graciously, Clouseau half-bowed. "Well, then . . . certainly."

"Inspector—it's been an honor."

And Boswell crisply saluted.

"Thank you," Clouseau said, and returned the salute, knocking himself in the head with the gas mask.

"I couldn't have done it without you, old chap," the spy said.

Just slightly groggy from the blow he'd delivered upon himself, Clouseau nonetheless beamed. "I know."

Then Boswell slipped away.

Just as Clouseau stepped from the secluded corner of the restaurant, the casino's security force burst in.

And as their eyes took in the brave man in the trenchcoat—with the gas mask in hand and gadgets poking from his pockets—smiles blossomed all around.

"You are a *hero!*" the chief of security said, rushing forward with open arms, the same formerly officious sort who had earlier given Ponton and Clouseau a hard time. "A true hero!"

"It was nothing," Clouseau shrugged, with a modest smile.

Then the paparazzi and news teams began to swarm in, to take pictures and video of the French detective who had come to Rome to nab the infamous Italian bandits. They had left their posts outside the casino to come inside and find a new celebrity, a real hero.

And Jacques Clouseau, true to his word, selflessly took all of the credit, bravely covering for his colleague in crime fighting.

It was the least he could do.

NINE

An Average Frenchman

In his spacious and exquisitely appointed salon, the President of France—his elegantly attired Justice Minister, Clochard, seated at his right hand—brought to order a committee meeting, whose outcome just days before would have seemed predictable indeed. But unpredictable events had suddenly steered the Medal of Honor committee down a most unexpected path.

"There is but one item on the agenda," the President said, standing at the head of a table filled with dignitaries. "It is our responsibility to give final approval to the list of nominees for our nation's highest award—the Medal of Honor."

All around the table, nods granted silent sanction to the President's words—only one of those seated did not nod, as it might seem self-aggrandizing to do so. Accordingly, Charles Dreyfus merely flashed a modest, overly rehearsed smile.

The President continued: "Only two names have been put forward this year, but both exemplify the highest standards of heroic service to our nation. It is, of course, a pity that of these deserving nominees, only one can receive this honor; but such is the nature of an award so esteemed."

More nods, and a diffident, practiced shrug from Dreyfus.

"The two nominees are Charles Dreyfus, Chief Inspector of the Police Nationale . . ."

Now it was the President's turn to nod, in recognition of Dreyfus, who waved a small humble hand.

". . . whom, you will no doubt recall, earlier this year smashed the Marseille cocaine cartel."

Polite applause around the table urged Dreyfus to respond, which he did, with a half-stand, half-bow.

"And Sister Marie-Hugette of the Ursuline Sisters, whose selfless concern for our nation's orphans is an inspiration to us all."

Again, polite applause followed, including Dreyfus (though his hands actually did not touch), who nodded with a smile of curdled warmth at the woman next to him, a heavy-set nun. The chief inspector thought, *If you are so self-less, why are you considering accepting this award?* The hypocrisy of some people, Dreyfus felt, was simply appalling.

Standing along the wall with other deputies, Renard gave his boss a discreet thumbs-up.

Clochard raised a tentative hand. "Monsieur President, if you will excuse me . . . Might I have the floor?"

Surprised eyes turned toward the Justice Minister, none more surprised than Dreyfus's.

"Certainly, Monsieur Clochard. The floor is yours."

The President sat; the Justice Minister stood.

"I would like to add one more name for the committee's consideration. I know we have reviewed many worthy candidates, and that this is a last-minute suggestion . . . but heroic service keeps to no timetable, certainly not a government committee's."

A mild ripple of amusement followed, although Dreyfus—who viewed Clochard through slitted eyes—took no part.

"I put forward Inspector Jacques Clouseau," Clochard began (initiating also a twitch at the corner of Dreyfus's left eye). "From a small village comes this simple man, previously unknown, to take on the most important investigation of our new century: the murder of our beloved Team France coach, Yves Gluant."

When France's famous soccer coach, Yves Gluant, is murdered and his most-prized possession— The Pink Panther Diamond—is stolen . . .

Gluant's pop-star girlfriend, Xania, should be suspect #1.

Her former boyfriend, soccer great Bizu, should be suspect #2 . . .

...and Chief Inspector Dreyfus of the Police Nationale should be on the case.

But fear that such a high-profile and difficult crime to solve will cost him his shot at the Medal of Honor leads Dreyfus to call bumbling Inspector Jacques Clouseau instead.

Has Dreyfus underestimated
the ever-klutzy Clouseau?

Even when his
hands are tied . . .

. . . Clouseau will shock,

play,

charm,

deceive,

smoke out,

and ultimately catch the culprit.

Then he'll snag the prize . . .

... and win hearts while he's doing it!

Heads lowered momentarily in respect to the late coach, even—reluctantly—Dreyfus's.

"Just last night, this officer so recently promoted to inspector captured the most notorious criminals in all of Europe—the so-called Gas-Mask Bandits."

To Dreyfus's horror, the President seemed clearly to be giving this suggestion serious thought. *But that was impossible!* Dreyfus thought. *Ridiculous . . . !*

But then the President said, "What an interesting idea—an average Frenchman, to rise overnight from obscurity to win the Medal of Honor."

"My thinking," Clochard said, with an openhanded shrug, "exactly."

Dreyfus, his eyes burning, did his best to conceal his feelings as his gaze traveled from committee member to committee member, only to find nods all around.

Dreyfus, forcing a smile, gestured with a dismissive hand. "No one is prouder of Clouseau than I—the man who discovered him and raised him to this elevated position."

"That is generous of you, Charles," Clochard said.

"But," Dreyfus said, sitting forward, "such an honor . . . if I may be allowed to express this opinion, without seeming to be self-serving . . . seems premature. His principal task is to find Coach

Gluant's killer . . . which in point of fact he has *not*. One might even say . . . to date, at least . . . he has been a disappointment, even a failure at this, his most important assignment."

Clochard nodded, shrugged, and said, "I do agree, Charles—he would only be considered if he finds the killer."

Along the sidelines, Renard was frowning.

"As it happens," Dreyfus said with an awkward smile, "I was, frankly, considering removing him from the case, and giving it to a more senior, qualified—"

"No, Chief Inspector," the President said, "I am sorry, but I must insist that you do not. You yourself, quite brilliantly, chose this humble hinterland investigator and presented him to a country that accepted him at once, warmly, as a national symbol. You must allow him to continue."

". . . Yes. Certainly, Monsieur President."

The President's expression took on a musing quality. "And just imagine—if he does manage to find Gluant's killer, and the Pink Panther itself . . . it might restore our nation's faith in this administration! The young voters, in particular."

Clochard said, "I am pleased, Monsieur President, that you see merit in my modest suggestion."

"It is an *excellent* idea, Clochard!" The President cast his eyes upon his committee. "All in favor?"

Every hand went up . . . even, at least, tremblingly, Dreyfus's, his eye twitching.

Clochard, seeing the twitch, misread it.

And winked back, thinking how generous the chief inspector had been.

As Dreyfus and Clochard returned to the Palais de la Justice—riding in the backseat of the chief inspector's chauffeured black Peugeot 607—kiosks on street corners displayed newspapers with headlines lauding Clouseau's remarkable feat at the Rome casino above a photo of the heroic inspector, chin high.

Inside the car, Dreyfus said, "That stupid face, looking at me, everywhere I go . . . How is it I was not informed of Clouseau going to that casino? What does this other idiot, Ponton, have to say for himself?"

Renard shrugged. "Merely that Clouseau took off on this wild goose chase, in the middle of the night, and did not wish to risk disturbing you."

"Well, I *am* disturbed! And you tell this clod Ponton I will accept *no* excuses . . . I want a report on Clouseau's whereabouts every hour, twenty-four hours a day! Tell him if he misses one call, he'll be walking a beat on the Belgium border! He misses *two* calls—he's off the force."

"I will tell him, sir."

As the Peugeot drew up in front of the Palais de la Justice, the vehicle was swarmed by reporters.

"Roll the window down, Renard," Dreyfus said.

"But, Chief Inspector—"

"We must treat the media with respect. They undoubtedly want to hear that my nomination for the Medal of Honor was formally made this morning."

Renard swallowed. "Yes, sir . . ."

The window went down, and the press swarmed up.

"Chief Inspector—how did Clouseau know to set his trap at the casino for the Gas-Mask Bandits?"

"Chief Inspector! Does Clouseau suspect the Gas-Mask Bandits may have engineered the Pink Panther theft?"

"Monsieur Dreyfus! Is Clouseau going to—"

With the tightest smile ever known to man, Dreyfus said, "Gentlemen . . . ladies! I cannot comment on an ongoing investigation . . ."

Below the sight line of the media, the chief inspector gestured frantically for the window to be rolled back up, which Renard did.

As the vehicle entered the Palais compound, Dreyfus muttered, "Must I do *everything* myself . . . ?"

Renard said nothing.

At the same time, after only a few hours' sleep, Inspector Clouseau was already at work, striding down a corridor toward his office. Just outside the door labeled INSPECTOR JACQUES CLOUSEAU, Ponton waited, like a patient palm tree.

Brightly, Ponton said, "Inspector, you will be pleased to know that I have rounded up everyone in Paris with the name 'You.' "

Clouseau frowned. "And you have done this why, my towering underling?"

"Because . . . you asked me to. Remember? Cherie Dubois reported the last words of Bizu: 'Oh, it's you?' "

The inspector straightened, beamed. "Yes, yes, I was merely testing you! Excellent work. Now we are *getting* somewhere. How many suspects have you rounded up?"

"One. A Mademoiselle Yu."

Seated in the same interrogation booth as had been the late Bizu, under a similarly harsh light, was an attractive Chinese woman in a red dress. She appeared utterly bewildered by why she was here.

Clouseau circled her, as a lion circles its prey, or a dog a tree.

Then, suddenly, he jabbed a forefinger in her startled face. "Where were *you*, Madam Yu, when Coach Gluant was murdered?"

Ponton, who had entered the booth with Clouseau, stepped out of the shadows to listen closely.

But all he heard was a long string of Chinese

words flying from the woman's lips, a rush of apparent invective that to his ears was gibberish. Clouseau's eyes were wide and seemingly uncomprehending as the sing-song chatter continued for what felt an eternity.

Finally, silence.

Clouseau rocked on his heels. His eyes narrowed, then widened again, then narrowed, then . . .

The inspector thrust his arm toward the door. "You . . . Yu . . . may go."

Ponton stuck his head into the hall, called for a gendarme, who escorted the woman out.

Then Ponton approached the inspector, asking gently, "Did you *get* any of that?"

"Of course!" Clouseau said, somewhat too indignantly.

"You speak . . . Chinese?"

"Of course I speak the Chinese!" Clouseau's eyes and nostrils flared. "Have I not told you I speak the dozen tongues? Are not two of them Cantonese and Mandarin?"

"Which was she speaking?"

"One of them! You are implying that I do not speak Chinese? Ah so, now Inspector Clouseau does not speak Chinese! Then what are we doing here? How could I not speak Chinese?"

As they walked to Clouseau's office, this continued for some time, Ponton saying nothing, Clouseau ranting, the assistant thinking that the inspector protested a bit too much . . .

* * *

Chief Inspector Charles Dreyfus's office was only one door down from Clouseau's, across the hall. So it was that Dreyfus—stung by the attention of the press, and the Medal of Honor committee, to this fool inspector—succumbed to temptation.

If this nincompoop Ponton would not report in regularly, Dreyfus himself would check up on the bumbler, Clouseau!

He knocked lightly at Clouseau's door.

No response.

He cracked the door open, peeked in.

No one within.

Soon he was prowling the office, snooping as only a great detective can snoop. He began with a filing cabinet of Clouseau's past cases, which had been shipped here from Fromage; but when the chief inspector pulled out the first drawer, it proved only half as long as usual, and—on well-oiled skids—flew out, and dropped, heavily, on Dreyfus's foot.

After performing a short, not terribly graceful dance, doing an effective mime of the pain that he actually felt, Dreyfus sat at Clouseau's desk, to get the weight off his crushed toes. Then he began to snoop some more, taking microfilm pictures of this and that, including all the pages in Clouseau's address book. He did not, however, take a picture of the contents of one drawer, which was devoted exclusively to mustache wax and dye.

Like an inviting meal, Clouseau's briefcase was set out on the desk just waiting for Dreyfus. He snapped it open and began to thumb through its contents, taking more microfilm pictures, the only sound the small clicks of the tiny camera.

But then came another sound, a loud obnoxious one: Clouseau's voice, across the hall, leaning in to speak to Dreyfus's secretary.

"Bon jour, Nicole!" Clouseau was saying. "Can you meet me in my office in a few minutes? I wish you to take the notes of my thoughts on the Gluant case."

Quickly, Dreyfus closed the curtains on the window nearest Clouseau's desk, and slipped behind them.

When Clouseau entered, he did not at first sense anything wrong. But when he sat at his desk, he knew at once that his briefcase was at the wrong angle and—most tellingly—the hair he had wedged within the closed right-hand drawer was gone.

His eyes lowered and he quickly spotted the strand of hair, plucked it from the floor and studied it between thumb and middle finger.

Thinking it through, Clouseau narrowed his eyes. Finally his mind reported its findings: *someone had opened that drawer!*

Something was . . . *amiss.*

He swivelled in the chair and saw the tips of brown shoes below the curtains, curtains he had not shut, shoes he did not own . . . *someone was behind there!*

Standing, Clouseau crossed to the door and opened it, calling, *"Nicole!* Could I see you now?"

He selected from several possibilities a fancy French chair (this was, after all, France) and he hefted it. Nicely solid.

Nicole slipped into the office, pad in hand, and saw Clouseau creeping toward the curtains, wielding the chair like a big bat. She squinted at him in confusion. "Yes, Inspector?"

"Ah, Nicole, my pet . . ." His eyebrows rose and so did the volume of his voice. *"Such very pleasant weather we are having. I was wondering if you think the weather, she is going to stay this mild . . ."*

Nicole's brow tensed further, as she said, "I, uh, certainly hope so, Inspector . . ."

Clouseau crept closer to the curtains. *"But do you think the weather, she is going to change?"*

"Let's keep our fingers crossed that it doesn't."

"Yes . . . yes, we will keep our fingers . . ."

And Clouseau swung the heavy chair into the curtains, smashing it into pieces on the person behind them.

". . . crossed!" Clouseau shouted triumphantly.

And Chief Inspector Dreyfus, his eyes open but not seeing anything, tumbled out from behind the curtains, flinging himself across Clouseau's desk draped like a dead moose on a proud hunter's fender.

Interestingly, the chief inspector wore a smile almost as surprised—and stupid—as the one Clouseau himself displayed.

Later that afternoon, Clouseau risked paying the chief inspector a visit.

He entered the office tentatively, saying, "Are you feeling better, Chief Inspector? I am so sorry, Chief Inspector. I did not imagine you would be springing the surprise inspector, Chief Inspection."

Dreyfus had been sitting on the edge of his desk, an ice bag to a swollen cheek, and sporting an elaborately blackened eye, which twitched now and then.

Now, seeing Clouseau, he got quickly behind the desk, to put something between him and the walking disaster that had just entered.

"The less said about it," Dreyfus said, "the better."

Clouseau beamed and approached the desk, stood with his hands locked behind him, rocking every so gently. "Good, good. I just thought I would drop by to give you the update on the case."

"Kind of you," Dreyfus said dryly.

Misinterpreting this, Clouseau became more casual; he sat on the edge of Dreyfus's desk, now that they were "buddies," not noticing the executive game of steel marbles, which when initiated would sway in "cause and effect" fashion. Right now they were at rest.

Like Clouseau.

Angled to look at his friendly colleague, Clouseau did notice something else on the desk: a collapsible pointer.

"Ah! I see you have the pointer that collapses, yes? Very useful, very handy! It is so much preferable to the pointing finger or the long wooden stick. With this . . ." And Clouseau lifted the pointer from the desk, regarding the thing expertly. ". . . one just *snaps* it open . . ."

Which he did, slapping Dreyfus in the face, though not noticing he had done so.

". . . and you are ready to go!"

Dreyfus, who had dropped his ice bag, recovered quickly, saying, "Well, then, Inspector. If you are ready to go—why don't you?"

"Ah, but the case, Chief Inspector!" Clouseau, closed the pointer, managing to hit no one, and tossed it on the desk, retaining his casual perch. "I must give you the report."

"Please."

"The case, she is going quite well, I am pleased to report."

"Splendid. If that's all—"

"Ah, but we just begin! You see, the crime, she has three components. *One*—the soccer stadium. *Two*—the people immediately surrounding the Coach Gluant. *Three*—the coach, his small circle of friends. And from this I have culled a list of the suspects key."

"Excellent," Dreyfus said, mildly surprised. "And how many suspects have you culled it down to?"

"Twenty-seven-thousand six-hundred and eighty-three."

Dreyfus drew in a deep breath; released it. Repeated: "Twenty-seven-thousand six-hundred and eighty-three. Suspects."

"That is right. From a city of millions, this culling I have done."

Dreyfus smiled. "Well, then—it sounds like only a matter of time. Tell me—have you *eliminated* any suspects?"

"Ha! Have I eliminated any suspects? You ask Clouseau if he has eliminated any suspects?"

"That's right. I believe I did ask you that."

"Well of course I have!"

"How many?"

"One."

Dreyfus swallowed thickly. "I see. And which suspect is that?"

Clouseau shrugged. "Gluant."

Dreyfus blinked, one eye blinking a bit more. "But Gluant . . . is the victim."

"Yes, of course. Excellent, Inspector. We think alike. We have ruled out the suicide." Finally Clouseau noticed the row-of-steel-marbles game, and said, "Oh, I like these, very much—the cause and the effect . . ."

He lifted the end ball bearing, and allowed it to swing back a good distance, released it, and sent the marbles flying and crashing and rolling around the desktop.

"Swine marbles . . ."

"That's all right," Dreyfus said, gesturing dismissively. "Just leave it."

"No, but such incompetence must be punished!"

"Really?"

"Yes! Yes! We must demand the refund from the manufacturer of this stupid game. Such shoddy workmanship! I will write a letter of the indignation!"

"Do that. Is there anything else?"

"No. I think we have covered, as the Americans say, the basis."

"Fine." Dreyfus flipped a little wave, returned to his paperwork. "Goodbye."

Clouseau nodded smartly, and went toward the door. Halfway there, he spun and asked, "Chief Inspector, you were at the game where the murder, she took place—were you not?"

Irritably, Dreyfus looked up. "Of course I was."

Walking back slowly, Clouseau spoke with deliberation. "I would request that you think back, Chief Inspector, and try to remember if you saw

anything suspicious that you may have overlooked reporting at the time . . ."

"Such as?"

"Seeing someone running around with a
poison-dart gun, perhaps?"

Dreyfus's smile was actually a grimace. "I will
think back and let you know."

Clouseau thrust a finger in the air, pointing at
the sky, or anyway, the ceiling. "I want to assure
you, Chief Inspector, that I will soon have your
killer . . . not *your* killer, you are quite alive, what
I mean to say is the killer that you *seek* . . . cor-
nered like the kangaroo in, in . . . the car . . . the
very small car!"

"Very well put," Dreyfus said dryly.

"Ah." Clouseau smiled in a conspiratorial
manner. "I see that you, too, take delight in the
play on the words. We have this in common, you
and I. The little . . . verbal joust. Charles . . . may I
call you 'Charles'?"

"No."

"Ah. Then I will call you 'Chief Inspector.' "

"Why don't you?" Dreyfus, suddenly feeling
he'd been too openly harsh, said, "I do appreciate
these comments. You have a . . . unique way with
words, a nice raconteur."

Clouseau frowned, not sure he understood, but
covered by saying, "I do know the nice 'rack' when
I see her, Chief Inspector, and may I take this opportunity to thank you for sharing Nicole with me."

"Why don't you get back on the job, Clouseau?"

"It has not progressed *that* far with Nicole, Chief Inspector, but I do appreciate that you do not have the priggish prejudice where the romance in the orifice, the *office*, she is concerned."

"Yes. Go. Just go."

Afraid he had been too familiar with his superior, Clouseau paused at the door and once again admired the elaborate filigree molding around its edges.

"Ah! I see you have decided to return this finely crafted molding to its original placement . . . a wise choice! I am of the perhaps controversial opinion that today's French craftspersons, they are every bit as skilled as those of the eighteenth century . . ."

As he spoke, Clouseau nervously fiddled with the filigree, and—again—it fell away in his hands.

Leaning the molding against the wall, Clouseau said, "I'll just leave it here . . . Looks very nice anywhere, really."

Dreyfus, alone at his desk now, did not know what to think. In a way, perhaps it was good that this man was such an utter idiot. Clouseau, with his tens of thousands of suspects, had no possibility of actually solving the Pink Panther case. But was the destruction the clown left in his wake really *worth* it?

As if his very desk were answering his question, the corner where Clouseau had perched collapsed, sending various items on the desk sliding toward the chief inspector, dumping themselves into his lap.

Reflexively, he rose, and cried out, *"Maintenance!"*

And, taking a step away from this latest Clouseau catastrophe, Chief Inspector Charles Dreyfus slipped on several of the ball bearings, causing the effect of him flying from his feet into the air—briefly—only to be deposited, rudely, on the floor behind his desk.

Clouseau, hearing the clatter from the hall, rushed back and stuck his head in. But there was no sign of the chief inspector at his desk, which was a terrible untidy mess.

As Dreyfus had apparently slipped out, Clouseau headed back to his office.

So many things to do. Unlike the chief inspector, Jacques Clouseau could hardly afford to just sit around at his desk, playing with his silly balls.

By late afternoon, the hours they had been keeping had taken a toll on both the inspector and his partner. They strolled together across a pedestrian bridge over the Seine, as the sun began to dip from sight, a cool lovely dusk settling over the City of Love.

In his now-famous trenchcoat, the man credited with capturing the Gas-Mask Bandits said to his burly associate, "To let the subconscious mind attack the case, while we sleep, let us once again go over the facts."

Ponton nodded. "Yves Gluant was killed at the International Championship Semi-Final."

"The murder!"

"In his neck was found a poison dart."

"The weapon!"

"His valuable ring, bearing the Pink Panther stone, was stolen in the melee."

"The robbery!"

"Near the victim at the time of his murder were his teammates, coaching staff and an estranged lover."

"The opportunity!"

"The star player Bizu had wished his coach dead, but has now been murdered himself."

"The complication!"

"Gluant was siphoning off money from his partner in their restaurant chain, casino owner Raymond Larocque."

"The motive!"

"But the person with the best motive, who was closest to the victim at the point of murder, was the estranged lover, Xania."

"The orgasm!"

Ponton stopped in his tracks. "What?"

"Ah, nothing, nothing, my strapping confederate." Clouseau paused and leaned against the stone bridge. "An excellent assembly of the facts. And from these we draw *what* inescapable conclusion?"

With a shrug, Ponton said, "That the singer Xania likely killed her lover, Yves Gluant."

Clouseau laughed and waved that off. "You poor callow creature—she is the obvious perpetrator, hence she is innocent."

The big man shook his head. "I tell you, Inspector, she *is* the killer! Please, I am only trying to help you . . . You are my partner, and now . . . my friend."

Clouseau, genuinely touched, said, "I do appreciate these words maudlin. But I do not believe that this gentle feminine flower, she has done this terrible thing."

Ponton's upper lip drew to reveal his teeth, but he wasn't smiling. "You do not want to see the truth, because you are emotionally involved! I could see it when the two of you were together at the recording studio—I could see a fool falling in love!"

Clouseau gave Ponton a sharp look. "You must not call Xania a fool! It is insulting and unkind—she cannot help her feelings, poor thing."

Shaking his head, sighing, Ponton said, "She is a *suspect*. You must regard her as such until such time as she has been cleared."

The inspector thought about that for several long moments, then said, "You are right! She may not be the killer, but I am convinced that she knows more than she is telling us, eh? And where is she now?"

Ponton smirked. "She left Paris suddenly—for America."

Eyes narrowing, Clouseau said, "It is a big place, my friend, but she cannot hide from us there."

"She isn't hiding—she's gone to New York, after she was told not to leave the city!"

"I see—she has gone the Apple Beeg to record? To make the video musique? To shoot the film?"

With heavy sarcasm, Ponton said, "No—on 'unspecified business.'"

Shrugging, Clouseau said, "Well, at least she had a good reason."

Ponton pressed. "Perhaps we should follow her to New York, Inspector . . . and see exactly what this 'business' is."

Clouseau shook his head. "No, Ponton, I will tell you what we will do—we will *follow* her to New York. And we will *see* exactly *what* this business *is!*"

Ponton just looked at him. Then he said, "Excellent idea, Inspector. Any other orders?"

"Just one—find me the greatest dialect coach in France! It is not enough to speak the English flawless—I must have the American accent, so as not to arouse suspicion."

Ponton frowned. "Do you really think that is *necessary*, Inspector . . . ?"

THE PINK PANTHER

"I do. Do you have any idea how they *feel* about the French over there right now?"

Ponton's eyes widened. "Good point, Inspector. But do you think the answer *is* in America? And as French police officers, can we even *make* an arrest in New York?"

The inspector put a hand on his charge's shoulder. "Ponton, if we can make it there," Clouseau said, "we can make it anywhere . . ."

Ponton was thinking about that when Clouseau charged him from his blind side, the large man stepping to one side to send the inspector over, catching him by the collar before the water could take him.

Dangling, Clouseau said, "Nice catch, Ponton! And now, let us do the same with the killer!"

TEN

Manhattan Malady

To Detective Second Class Gilbert Ponton, Inspector Jacques Clouseau remained something of an enigma—a clumsy, bumbling enigma, to be sure; but an enigma nonetheless.

It seemed that only two assumptions were made by those around Clouseau—that he was an unparalleled hero, an investigative genius, which his capture of the Gas-Mask Bandits seemed to support; or an absolute boob, a fool of the first order, as Chief Inspector Dreyfus assumed (and as much of what Ponton himself had observed would seem to indicate).

And yet.

There were times when Ponton wondered if

this idiot might not be an idiot savant—he had a detective's instincts, and certain abilities, a flair for foreign languages among them, though Ponton doubted the ever-increasing list of "tongues" the inspector claimed to have mastered.

And Clouseau truly was brave, if stupidly so at times. His frequent attacks upon Ponton, a much larger man, were indications of the foolhardy inspector's enormous, possibly misguided, self-confidence.

Now they were in New York, on the streets of Manhattan, and at a sidewalk stand Clouseau was ordering a hamburger—in an over-exaggerated, but admittedly thoroughly American, accent . . . which had only taken the inspector a full day to master ("hamburger" for many hours having been something along the lines of "hum-bearg-air").

They had arrived yesterday, and Clouseau's accent had been so convincing when they had checked into their hotel—La Sofitel—that the French desk clerk had muttered to himself in their native tongue, "stupid American," not knowing Clouseau (and Ponton) understood.

What had followed was one of those moments that made Ponton wonder: Clouseau had had trouble with the pen provided at check-in, and requested a loan of the personal pen of that clerk (later privately referred to by the inspector as the "swine clerk").

When the patronizing, sneering clerk had complied, Clouseau continued to fill in the registration forms, and then handed back the pen . . . which the clerk put in his breast pocket, unaware that an ink blot had begun immediately to blossom there. Clouseau called back, grinning, in his most exaggerated American accent, "Have a good one!"

Stupidity on Clouseau's part?

Or cunning?

Ponton could never quite be sure. All he knew was that he felt guilty over reporting to Renard and Dreyfus behind his partner's back. Last night, sharing the double bed the "swine clerk" had provided them, the two men had talked in the dark, like the old friends they were beginning to be.

Clouseau had admitted an attraction to Xania, but had said, "True love, my friend? It has not yet come Clouseau's way. I, uh . . . never see *you* with the women?"

Ponton, realizing that he was one of two men sharing a single bed, had said reassuringly—and truthfully: "I am married, Inspector."

"But I see no ring."

"If the criminals of the underworld knew I was married, my wife, my Marie, she might be in danger."

"Ah! So wise. You are not the fool you at times seem, Ponton. You must love her very much."

"I do. To me, she is the most desirable woman in the world. And you?"

"I have never met your wife, but I am sure she is—"

"No, I mean . . . is there a woman besides Xania in your life? Nicole, perhaps?"

"Ah, Nicole . . . such a sweet, innocent child."

Ponton, remembering the positions he'd seen Clouseau and the secretary share, had said gently, "But you seem so . . . intimate."

"She is my pupil, like you, my friend. A naif in the ways of the world. Could a simple soul such as her keep up with the career, the life, the passions of Clouseau? This I doubt, very much."

"Well, it *is* hard."

In the darkness a few seconds passed before Clouseau had responded: ". . . uh, *what* is hard?"

"To meet the woman, in the life we lead. The life of danger. The hours so long."

"Ah, Ponton, you are learning. You are learning."

Indeed Ponton *was* learning: within moments he had deflected Clouseau's shot in the dark and punched him in the stomach.

"*Oooh!* . . . Good night, Ponton, my vigilant friend."

"Good night."

"That hurt, you know."

"If you attack me in my sleep, Inspector, the next one will hurt more."

Clouseau had chuckled, or was that a whimper? "No, I think we have enough of the lesson tonight, my big little star pupil, star pupil . . ."

Now that they'd eaten a quick lunch as they walked the busy sidewalks of Manhattan, Ponton strode happily along with Inspector Clouseau. They were on their way to Xania's hotel, the Waldorf. Ponton had used his laptop computer in their room at the Sofitel to make a computer check of the singer's phone records—from New York to France and back to New York, the cyber trace went . . . revealing two phone calls she had made to a certain jeweler—a Simon Sykorian.

As they strolled along on this sunny day, Ponton reported these new findings; Clouseau, after taking it all in (Ponton hoped), asked, "This Sykorian, if he is a jeweler, why is this suspicious? Certainly a lovely woman like Xania has a right to adorn herself with the jewel."

Though he used the American accent only when called for, the inspector insisted upon English while in New York, with Clouseau's unique French accent and word-mangling patois making the trip.

"Ah, but Sykorian is a notorious scoundrel, Clouseau."

Nodding sagely, Clouseau asked, "Have you noticed this, Ponton? How many of these scoundrels, they are also notorious?"

"Uh, yes. Anyway, he's a black market diamond cutter."

Clouseau stopped dead. "Do not tell me . . ."

"Yes. The Pink Panther, our nation's most revered symbol of wealth and power, could be carved up in smaller pieces, for fencing purposes."

"I asked you not to tell me!"

"There's the Waldorf. Let us cross here, Inspector, and—"

Clouseau's arm gripped Ponton's. "No. You must not walk as the jay! They are very strict about their laws traffique . . . We will go to the corner and remain inconspicuous."

They waited with other pedestrians for the red hand, indicating STOP, to turn to green; only it was not green, rather white, a bent-over crooked figure indicating WALK. To indicate to Ponton his strict compliance with the American traffic regulations, Clouseau crossed in that same distorted posture.

Ponton thought, *Fool . . . clown . . . eccentric? Who can know?*

When they reached the Waldorf, Xania—as if on cue—emerged, looking stunning in a white dress that complemented her creamy chocolate complexion and showed off her full bosom nicely. The only nod toward keeping a low profile was her floppy creamy brown hat with a white band, a blue purse slung over one arm.

Clouseau took Ponton's elbow and whispered: "Perhaps she will take us to this notorious scoundrel. We will shadow her . . ."

"But she *knows* us, Inspector!"

Keeping the singer in his sight, Clouseau stopped at a newsstand and purchased two tabloids. He handed one to Ponton, keeping the other for himself.

"The newspaper ploy," Clouseau explained, with a wicked little smile.

As they followed the beautiful woman, they covered their faces with newspapers. To Ponton's consternation, Clouseau insisted upon reverting to the distorted "walking man" posture when they crossed at pedestrian lights; hardly Ponton's idea of staying inconspicuous . . .

Nonetheless, Xania apparently did not make them, and within half an hour she had led them onto a side street where warehouses faced each other glaringly. The sophisticated Manhattan ambience had shifted suddenly into a film noir nightmare of suspicious vans, shoddy storefronts and seedy characters.

"And so," Clouseau said, lowering his newspaper, "we are in that most famous of criminal districts, an area notorious for crime . . ."

Ponton lowered his tabloid, as well. "And what is that, Inspector?"

Clouseau flashed him a darkly meaningful

glance. "The . . . Warehouse District! . . . *Newspapers!*"

The detectives snapped their newspapers protectively in place, Xania having paused to look back over her shoulder. They continued to follow her thusly, until Clouseau inadvertently fell down the stairs into a subway entry.

But he emerged none the worse for wear on the opposite stairs, just as Xania was rounding the next corner.

When Clouseau and Ponton came around that same corner, however, she had disappeared; but the clip-clop of her high heels alerted them to where she had gone: the nearest warehouse. They slipped inside, via a loading dock, and found themselves standing before a bank of freight elevators, one of them already rising—most likely, with the beautiful object of their surveillance in it.

Clouseau pointed to the elevator floor indicator: 12.

"That is our destination," the inspector said to his assistant. Then he frowned. "As the American argot has it, I smell something . . . fishy."

"We did pass two fish markets," Ponton said helpfully, jerking a thumb behind him.

"No, I make the play on the words. Here—perhaps we should take the stairs, not the elevator."

But before they could make that decision, another of the elevators came to rest, a slatted wooden door swung up, and out stepped three tall, muscular men wearing dark, tight suits, sunglasses and sneers.

The nearest one, a craggy-faced character, snarled, "What's your business here?"

Clouseau and Ponton exchanged glances as the trio approached. That their eyes were shielded by the opaque lenses made them all the more menacing.

Summoning his best American accent, Clouseau asked, "We're looking for a diamond cutter."

"There's no diamond cutter in this building."

"Not even of the . . . black market variety?"

The craggy-faced man's sneer grew and his hand slipped inside his suitjacket.

Clouseau threw a karate chop that dropped the man, and the fight was on, Ponton taking out one with a flip over his shoulder, sending the brute sprawling to the cement, Clouseau mostly chopping the air with bladed hands but making occasional contact, ducking all blows, Ponton taking the remaining two out at the same time, with a punch and a kick.

The trio lay unconscious on the floor; it was so quick they still wore their sunglasses, though one lens was spider-webbed.

"This is what they call in America," Clouseau said, "the Welcome Wagon."

"They seem to have fallen off it," Ponton observed.

"You did very well! Very well! You see, my substantial sidekick! These lessons, these surprise attacks . . . they pay off!"

They rode up the freight elevator, which stopped at the sixth floor.

Clouseau frowned at Ponton. "We make the unscheduled stop . . . Vigilance, my friend. Vigilance."

Two Asian men, burly, sinister of face, in tasteless sportshirts and tight trousers, stepped aboard. One took Clouseau's side, the other Ponton's. The Asians stared at the two detectives with openly threatening expressions.

The tension mounted as the elevator rose, seventh floor, eighth floor, ninth . . .

"Now, Ponton!" Clouseau said, as he executed a karate chop to the belly of the Asian nearest him.

Ponton grabbed the man at his side and thrust him into the wall of the elevator, its wood and steel clattering.

But these two were not pushovers, and the fight on the elevator was a brutal thing, its participants bouncing off the walls and each other, an exchange of savage blows, some missing, some connecting . . .

When the elevator reached the twelfth floor, however, the two Asian "swine" were in a pile, out cold, like the sunglassed thugs who'd dared assault the French detectives below.

Ponton sent the unconscious men down, and joined Clouseau in the open loft, where various work and storage areas were interspersed. Way across the room, opposite the elevators, a small, rather nondescript, fifty-ish man with a jeweler's loupe over his right eye, and in white shirtsleeves and dark apron, sat at a work station while Xania, distinctive in the floppy light-brown hat and stark white dress, stood watching.

The man, obviously the jeweler Sykorian, had a small saw in hand, and it was buzzing, as he leaned over a glittering object in a vise.

"Like the ice you will freeze!" Clouseau demanded.

Xania looked sharply toward them, as did the jeweler, who removed the loupe to give the attention of both his eyes to these intruders.

The detectives strode over, Clouseau saying, "Stop what you are doing! And you need not try to flee—you are defenseless! We have already put out of the commission your thugs of the strongarm!"

By this time they were all but on top of the jeweler—an average-looking fellow but for his slitted, hard gaze and a harsh, full-lipped mouth that right now was scowling.

"*What* thugs?" he asked, with more confusion than indignation.

"Do not bother playing the game! Your bodyguards, these men strong of back and weak of mind who you have patrolling this building!"

"There's no security here," the jeweler said, with a little shrug, "until nightfall. There's not much at all going on in this building right now—just the sunglasses shop and the Chinese carry-out joint."

"Ah." Clouseau turned to Ponton and whispered, "You may owe someone an apology, my impulsive friend."

Ponton, ignoring that, displayed his badge to the jeweler. "Sorry to interrupt you . . . but what *exactly* are you cutting there?"

"What does it look like? A diamond—pink. Seven carats. Clear. Why?"

Clouseau thrust himself forward. "Clear? There is no flaw at the center? Of a bist that is lipping?"

"A what that is what?"

"A bist that she is lipping! A lipping bist! A lipping bist, you fool."

Xania, matter of fact, explained: "A leaping beast. He thinks this is the famous Pink Panther."

The jeweler laughed humorlessly. "Don't be ridiculous. This is a clear stone—a gift from the French Minister of Justice for his new mistress. I am to provide a setting."

Clouseau's eyes narrowed. "And why would the Minister of France come to you, a jeweler in New York, to provide the setting for him and his mistress in which to play?"

"No, you imbecile—it's a setting for the jewel! I'm to set it."

Ponton was leaning over, examining the diamond in the small vise. "He tells the truth. This is not the Pink Panther."

Clouseau, his pride ruffled, turned to Xania, chin high. "And what are you doing here, sneaking around like the naughty schoolgirl who needs the spanking? Why have you left Paris?"

From the diamond cutter's desk nearby, Xania lifted a small clutch purse, a dark little thing studded with diamonds and stunning in its ornate deco design.

"Mr. Sykorian is the best at what he does," she explained, with a smile even more dazzling than the diamonds in the fancy purse she displayed. "This is a valuable, priceless item, and only *he* could properly repair it."

Clouseau said, "I see. And what is it that makes this purse so priceless?"

She lifted an eyebrow casually. "It once belonged to Josephine Baker."

Clouseau's eyes popped open. "*Mon dieu . . .*" He crossed himself, and Ponton felt himself melt inside, at the name of the renowned entertainer, beloved by all of France.

"It was a gift to her in nineteen fifty-seven," Xania said, and then dropped her second bomb: "Given to Josephine Baker by . . . Jerry Lewis."

Clouseau dropped to his knees, and hung his head, and held out prayerfully clasped hands, beseeching her, "Forgive, my dear! Forgive me for doubting you . . ."

Ponton, moved himself, lifted his partner to his feet and provided a handkerchief for Clouseau to dry his eyes.

Xania was offhandedly explaining, "The purse was falling apart—each of these diamonds is precious, and must be firmly in place before tomorrow night."

Clouseau, his poise nearly regained, asked, "And what is 'tomorrow'?"

"The Presidential Ball. In Paris."

His brow tensed. "But you are in New York . . ."

"And tomorrow I'll fly back to Paris. You *did* say I needed to stay available in Paris . . ."

Clouseau beamed at her. He took one of her hands in both of his. "And I knew I could count on you, my darling suspect."

Ponton, less charmed, asked, "Why did you arrange to see a black market diamond cutter for such a job?"

She flashed an irritated look at Ponton, snapping, "I told you—Sykorian is the best!" Then she returned her features to an innocent cast as she said to Clouseau, "I had no idea he had this other, underground reputation."

The jeweler said, "It's slander. My record is flawless . . . like my work."

"But not like the Pink Panther, eh? Which has its distinctive flaw."

"Yes, I know—a 'lipping bist.' "

Clouseau took Xania aside. "My dear, why did you not tell Clouseau you were leaving . . . and the innocent reason behind it?"

She batted long eyelashes at him. "Well, just look at the fuss you've made! With the Pink Panther stolen, how could I go to a diamond dealer without arousing suspicion?"

"I must admit," Clouseau said, "you *did* arouse me . . ."

The phone on the diamond cutter's desk rang.

Clouseau held up a hand, and went to the ringing phone. "I will answer it. It may be one of your unscrupulous clients, Monsieur Skyroian, who will want some of the black market work done . . . and we will see how long your reputation, it remains spotless!"

Answering, Clouseau said, "Yes?"

Ponton watched in rapt anticipation . . .

"Yes," Clouseau said, "you raise the point interesting, monsieur . . . No, no, no . . . I did not *know* these things!"

Clouseau and Ponton traded significant, sly smiles.

"Yes . . . yes. That *does* sound like a steal . . . Yes, let us go through with this scheme. As it happens . . . I am *not* happy with my phone service! I will take the plan five-year."

Ponton sighed and watched the floor while Clouseau gave the operator his credit card information, then hung up.

"No one can say Clouseau did not accomplish anything here this afternoon!" the inspector said. "I believe I just made the deal very shrewd . . ."

Again the phone rang, but this time Ponton held up his hand, saying, "Let the machine take it."

"Ah, yes," Clouseau said. "Let the mysterious client leave the massage."

The jeweler frowned. "The what?"

"Quiet, you fool!"

The voice on the machine had a European accent that Ponton could not quite place. *"The 'animal' is out of its cage. And since you are the world's greatest 'trainer,' it will find its way to you . . . in good time. Call me."*

The machine clicked off.

"Well," Ponton said with satisfaction. "It is obvious that whoever that was has the Pink Panther!"

The jeweler looked at the nearest wall, his face an expressionless mask.

Clouseau chuckled patiently, and took Ponton's face in his hands like that of an adorable child. "My silly, silly goose of a pupil. Sometimes the hot dog, she is merely the hot dog, the train tunnel, only the train tunnel, the two large balloon, only the two large balloon. Clearly this massage was in regard of an animal that had escaped from her cage. Nonetheless . . ."

The inspector thrust a pointing forefinger at the jeweler. "This answer-massage machine, she must not leave town! Is this understood?"

The jeweler's eyes did not in fact register understanding, but he said just the same, "Uh . . . sure. Why not."

Clouseau accompanied Xania as they left the warehouse, Ponton trailing, feeling somewhat shellshocked. As they reached the street, an ambulance was loading in gurneys bearing the trio of men in sunglasses and the two Asians from the earlier encounters.

"This *is* a rough neighborhood," Xania said, and clutched Clouseau's arm.

"Yes, my dear, in this savage American city," Clouseau said, "the senseless violence, she is around every corner . . . Would you excuse me for a small moment?"

"Of course . . ."

Clouseau took Ponton aside and whispered, "I see that you were correct, my cunning friend— she knows much that she does not tell us. For example, what time is her plane leaving tomorrow?"

Ponton blinked. "Why not just ask her?"

"Too obvious. I need her to be inside of my confidence, and I to be inside of . . . her."

Ponton frowned. "What . . . ?"

Clouseau leaned even closer. "I believe the seduction ploy, she is called for."

"Why don't you just *ask* her?"

"But then she may be deceptive, whereas if I pump her for the information . . ."

Xania approached. "Uh, Inspector? Is there any chance you'd like to join me tonight, for dinner at the Waldorf?"

"Of course, mademoiselle! But my friend Ponton, he is busy this evening. He has the many museum to visit."

Ponton frowned. "I do? . . . I mean, I do."

Clouseau, stepping away from his partner, taking Xania by the arm, asked, "And what time, my dear?"

"Say . . . eight o'clock?"

He shrugged. "Eight o'clock."

"Say . . . in my room, on the second floor?"

"In my room, on the second floor."

"No . . . *my* room."

"Oh. Yes, of course, your room."

She smiled at him, with a wattage even the Pink Panther might well envy. "I'll see you there, then."

Clouseau, trembling, swallowed and managed, "Yes. Yes. There you will see me. You will see me there. There I will be seen . . ."

The devil was in her smile as she walked down the street, chocolate legs swishing under the white ice-cream dress, to hail a taxi.

Ponton was at Clouseau's side, as the inspector said, "You see, my sizeable subordinate? She plays into my hands like the putty."

"It could be a trap," Ponton cautioned.

"It *is* a trap! It is *Clouseau's* trap . . . She is the rat, and I am the cheese!"

Ponton nodded. "That sounds about right."

ELEVEN

Cause for Alarm

Inspector Jacques Clouseau, after a brief fifteen-minute sojourn in the "swine revolving door," entered the lavish lobby of the Waldorf Hotel. He wore his trademark trenchcoat and a small, anticipatory smile. *Tonight*, he thought, his eyes taking in the glitter of the impressive chandelier that seemed to sparkle with possibilities, *is the night* . . .

Xania met him at the door to her suite on the second floor, a suite only slightly smaller—and possibly more lavish—than the lobby itself; with its white walls and golden-upholstered plush furnishings, all that was missing was that enormous chandelier.

The singer still wore the same lovely white dress as this afternoon, and apologized: "I've had a busy day . . . I hope you don't mind. We'll just be informal and—"

He held up a traffic-cop palm and raised a "shush" finger to his lips.

Raising his voice a notch, he said, *"Such very pleasant weather we are having . . . I hope this blissful weather, she continues . . ."*

Soon Xania got the drift, as her guest prowled the large living room of the exquisite suite, checking behind chairs, curtains, even in the fireplace.

Then he curled a finger in "come" fashion and she stepped close to him. He whispered: "We are indeed alone, my dear . . . but I must still check for the boogs."

"Boogs?"

"Boogs. The little tiny listening devices with eyes that spy upon what we say."

"Oh. Sure."

And now the inspector brought his expert touch to sweeping the room for surveillance equipment, his fingers skimming the tops of doors, tripping nimbly along floorboards, looking in lamps, inspecting telephones, all in all a process that took a good five minutes while Xania, arms folded across her full bosom, watched with interest and, perhaps, amusement.

The floor was parquet, covered by various expensive throw rugs. Beneath an Oriental carpet

Clouseau made a shocking discovery: a large metal plate screwed tight into the wood.

Xania began, "Did you find—"

Clouseau frowned and motioned her over, to share his unnerving find. He slipped an arm around her, drew him to her and, her Chanel in his nostrils, his eyes plunging to her plunging neckline, he whispered into her ear: "It is a large boog indeed. Say nothing. You are in the best of hands."

She gave him a teasing look. "I hope to be."

He waggled a finger. "Naughty girl, naughty, naughty . . ."

He knelt over the blatant listening device—what sort of fool did they take him for?—and examined the screws and wires, some of which held the devil in place, others of which no doubt served to enable electronic eavesdropping. He got out his Swiss Army knife, opened it, did not hurt himself, and deftly cut the wires, and began to carefully, gingerly unscrew the plate, listening and watching, just in case the trap for the boob had been laid . . .

He gestured for her to stand away as he leaned in and ever so slowly unscrewed the final screw . . .

He stood. "There—that should do it."

"What's that . . . *grinding* sound?"

Shrugging, Clouseau put the carpet back in place. "I hear nothing."

"Metal against wood—don't you hear it?"

The sound that followed was enormous—a shattering, earth-shaking crash, after which several shrill screams, muffled by the floor, could nonetheless be clearly heard.

"I heard *that*," Clouseau admitted, having no idea that he had just caused the enormous chandelier to plunge into the middle of the lobby and shatter into shards on the floor.

She went to his arms and clung to him. "What could it have been?"

"Mice perhaps? The mouse, he scurries across the floor, and the woman, she screams. So silly, to be frightened of the mouse."

Xania's eyes were large. "Well, that sounded like *some* mouse . . ."

He shrugged. "This is after all New York. They have the pestilence problem, even at the fine hotel . . . Shall we call for the service of the room?"

Soon, having enjoyed a delicious lobster dinner, they sat by candlelight at a small room-service cart/table, Xania sipping a glass of wine, Clouseau boldly drinking his flaming glass of mojito.

"An unusual drink," Xania observed.

"It was introduced to me," Clouseau said with a suave wave, "by a close friend and colleague . . . in the Secret Service of England."

"Do you ever get burned?"

"Only in love, my dear . . . Only in love . . ."

She sipped her wine, smiling just a little. "Sometimes I don't know what to make of you, Inspector."

"Make of me what you will."

She shrugged a trifle. "I mean, you're . . . a man of mystery."

"Well, I am a man who solves the mysteries, this is true. But one mystery I cannot solve."

"Yes?"

He leaned nearer her. "Why were you so elusive today?"

"What do you mean?"

"You walked many blocks from this hotel to that shabby district of the warehouse. My partner Ponton and I, we followed you."

"I know. Behind those newspapers."

She rose from the little table and sat on a nearby sofa, patting the cushion beside her—*right* beside her.

Clouseau rose and sat where she had indicated, saying, "You did not mind that your tail we followed?"

"No. I'm not afraid of you." Her smile was mischievous; then it disappeared. "But I *am* afraid of Raymond Larocque."

Clouseau frowned. "Has he threatened you, this swine Larocque?"

"Not directly, but he has sent out word on the street, threatening to kill *anyone* in possession of the Pink Panther. He believes it is rightfully his."

"Yes. Your late friend Gluant owed him much money. But why, of the many suspects of this theft, would he follow *you*, my sweet?"

Her eyelashes fluttered. "Well, after all, I was in New York to see a diamond cutter. He might have jumped to the wrong conclusion."

He bestowed his most debonair smile. "You know, a man sitting next to you, in your private suite . . . he might jump to the wrong conclusion, also."

"Or . . ." She reached a slender hand across the table and touched his. ". . . the right one. I have heard things about you."

"That, for example, I am French?" He leaned in sideways to sip his mojito from the nearby room-service table, the back of his hair catching fire, just a little, providing a low blue flame that neither he nor his lady friend noticed.

"That you know how to treat a woman." She touched her breasts, a hand on either. "Would you like to touch them . . . ?"

"Oh yes. Very much."

She blinked. "Why don't you then?"

"Oh. Oh! Yes . . . I will touch them."

And he did. He murmured into her ear, "The heat of your love . . . it burns me. I am aflame with desire . . ."

"And now," she said, with a wicked smile, a hand sliding down his midsection, "I will touch *you* . . ."

He sprang to his feet. "And so the games of love, they begin. If you will let me slip away, my darling . . . to prepare . . . for the making of the love."

Clouseau backed away from her, blowing kisses that she returned; that the back of his hair was aflame had not yet registered on either of them.

His back to the bathroom door, he gazed at her with his sexiest French one-eyebrow-cocked come-hither look, then sniffed the air, and asked, "Do you smell burning rubber, my pet? . . . No matter."

Her lips pursed sensuously; her eyes were half-lidded; and her voice was a purr as she said, "I will slip into something special for you, Jacques, and meet you back here . . . on the couch . . ."

"This is a rendezvous I will kept, my sweet Xania . . ."

Within the bathroom, Clouseau reached desperately into his pockets. He had a small problem. The stresses of being a great detective had taken a big toll. And so finally he found the tiny vial, which was marked VIAGRA—EXTRA STRENGTH.

He opened the bottle and saw the single precious pill within. *I must renew that prescription*, he thought. *Perhaps I should make the note . . .*

He shook the little blue pill into his left palm. Then he put down the vial, picked the pill up in thumb and middle finger, and lifted it to gaze upon as if it were as precious a jewel as the Pink Panther itself; and in the mirror, he saw that his hair was on fire.

He yelped, jumping with surprise and pain, and the little pill took a trip—it made a high journey into the air, just missing the ceiling, did a somersault, and performed a perfect dive into the sink, rolling down the drain.

Clouseau could not react to this with the proper horror until he had put his hair out; patting the flames away with a towel, he sighed—he felt fine, no burning—and he lifted the vial, realizing finally that his only pill had gone down a pipe as straight and stiff as he was not.

Frantically, he read the label: REFILLS: ONE.

He peeked out the bathroom door and saw Xania returning from her bedroom in a sheer blue nightie. He stared at her lush, curvaceous beauty; then down at himself.

Nothing.

And if that sight didn't do it, then only a refill would . . .

On the room service cart, pushed away from where Xania reclined in all her glory on the couch, that mojito was flaming high now. Best get rid of that.

He tiptoed into the room, unseen as he snatched the out-of-control drink from the table, and—as Xania lay in a light slumber, awaiting her lover, moving sensually with the thought of delights to come—Clouseau crept from the hotel suite, grabbing his trenchcoat as he went.

By the time he got to the lobby, he had the trenchcoat on, and the mojito's flames were leaping higher. Casually he dumped the drink into a potted tree, and moved quickly through the lobby, in and around maintenance men who were clearing out a formidable pile of broken glass from the lobby floor. Whatever could *that* have been?

Out on the street, his empty pill bottle tight in his hand, he ran to the nearest pharmacy; but just as he went to enter, the druggist turned a CLOSED sign toward him. Frantically, Clouseau held up the vial, pounding on the glass with his fist, his eyes pleading. The druggist shrugged and disappeared into the store, shutting off lights as he went.

By the time Clouseau had reached the third pharmacy—slowed up just a little by the need to cross the crosswalks in the proper posture—he realized that time was running out. Sweet Xania would notice his absence, and when he finally returned, he would have explaining to do, with only the flimsiest of excuses.

Like all detectives, Clouseau knew that even the best of men, when pushed to the wall, could turn to crime; and he was no exception.

From his trenchcoat pocket he took Secret Agent Boswell's glass-cutting device with its attached suction cup. Looking all around, finding this side street empty of anything but parked cars and damp pavement, he went to work on the glass with the cutter, the cup securely attached.

Soon his work was complete.

And the glass around the square he had cut fell to the pavement, shattering all around him, leaving him standing there with a square of glass attached to his suction cup.

Nonetheless, five minutes later, now wearing a Waldorf robe, Clouseau slipped out of the bathroom, having taken *two* little blue pills, just to be sure . . .

In her provocative pose, Xania lay back on the couch like a pin-up come magically to life. Her lovely lipsticked lips parted to say, "You *do* like to keep a girl waiting . . . oh! What is it you have *there!*"

"It is all part of the game of love," he said, and dropped the robe. It caught on something, then he flicked it to the floor and stood there naked as the day he was born, except for the t-shirt, boxer shorts and black socks.

He sat on the edge of the couch. Her eyes were wide on what he had brought to the game. He moved in to kiss those succulent red-rouged lips, which parted, a pink tongue flicking . . .

The fire alarm shocked both of them out of the moment, jostled them literally off the sofa and onto the floor.

The intercom voice was mechanical and commanding: *"Fire alert. This is not a drill. Repeat, this is not a drill. Exit the building at once, using marked exits. Exit the building at once . . ."*

He reached for his robe, but the mechanical voice scolded him: *"Take no time to grab your things! This is not a drill!"*

Clouseau grabbed the lovely young woman up into his arms, as if carrying a bride across the threshold and—the inspector clad only in t-shirt, boxers and socks, Xania in her sheer nightie—they quickly made their exit.

She dropped to her feet in the hall, took his hand, and they ran down the stairs into and through the lobby, where firemen were fighting the blaze that had risen from the potted plant where Clouseau had deposited his flaming mojito. Other firemen directed them toward the front of the building.

Within moments they were standing in the street, hundreds of guests from the hotel stranded out there, many in their robes, still others staring at the man in his boxers next to the incredibly beautiful young woman in the nightie.

Soon virtually everyone was staring at Clouseau, or at least at a part of Clouseau, including several envious horses at their carriages.

"By the way," he said to Xania idly, "what time does your flight leave tomorrow?"

"Ten a.m.," she said.

"Ah. Thank you."

And when the firemen had cleared the lobby and informed the guests that they might return to their rooms, she led him back to her suite.

Not by the hand.

TWELVE

Hero's Homecoming

Once again Chief Inspector Charles Dreyfus met in his spacious office with his team of top investigators, as they—and he—shared their findings. On an easel was a giant blow-up of a surveillance photo, depicting a distinguished-looking Asian individual.

"Gentlemen," Dreyfus said, standing beside the photo and nodding to it, "meet Dr. Li How Pang—director of China's Ministry of Sport. This was taken just before Coach Gluant was murdered—Dr. Pang was seated in the nearby VIP box. Now . . . coincidentally . . . when Gluant was last in Beijing, he took several meetings with the good Dr. Pang . . ."

Dreyfus moved along to the next of half a dozen other such displayed surveillance-photo enlargements. In one, Coach Gluant and Pang were exchanging smiles and shaking hands.

"This was taken on that very same Beijing trip," Dreyfus said, and gestured decisively toward the image with his collapsible pointer. Unfortunately, the instrument had not recovered from its meeting with Inspector Clouseau and the thing fell apart with the motion, clattering in pieces to the floor, leaving Dreyfus holding two small fragments. He tossed these away casually and pointed with his finger.

He did not notice—although his deputy Renard did—that several of the top detectives present exchanged wary glances. They had noticed, of late, that Dreyfus seemed off his game; for all of the confidence the chief inspector displayed, something ragged remained out at the edges—take that ever-growing tic at his left eye, for example.

Dreyfus was saying, "In fact, an examination of Dr. Pang's subsequent budget requisitions and Gluant's bank statements would indicate that they entered into an arrangement whereby Pang would deposit in an account of Gluant's large sums of money . . . money diverted from the Sports Ministry."

Dreyfus, as he spoke, moved along to other blow-up displays of the evidence—Chinese government documents complete with yen amounts underlined and dates highlighted, juxtaposed with Coach Yves Gluant's bank deposit records, similarly underlined and highlighted, showing yen turning into Euros.

"Presumably," Dreyfus continued, "the coach was to invest these sums on Pang's behalf. Other records, however, indicate that Gluant was less than good at his word . . ."

The chief inspector moved to the next blow-up display: casino account records.

"Our esteemed coach had a very bad habit for a person in his profession," Dreyfus said with grim confidence. "From the inquiries *you* have made, gentlemen, we now know that Yves Gluant was a compulsive gambler."

Renard, from the sidelines, was relieved to see the investigators again regarding Dreyfus with obvious respect and admiration.

"It becomes painfully apparent," Dreyfus said, "that Gluant took Pang's money and gambled it away . . . knowing full well that Pang had no recourse, that one cannot step forward to press charges against a thief who has squandered away funds *first* stolen away by the accuser himself!"

Satisfied nods all around the room.

"Think of the danger Pang was in, from his own government!" Dreyfus shrugged. "Execution would only be the end game—the torture that would precede it, well . . . you are men of the international community, you understand."

Knowing smiles blossomed, now.

"So we have a man with not just one motive, but two—Pang could take revenge upon the creature who had swindled and betrayed him; and at the same time, from the very finger of this same unsavory victim, Pang could pluck a single ring with a single stone, that could solve all of his financial miseries!"

Now nods *and* smiles . . .

Dreyfus, even if deprived of his pointer, became emphatic and dramatic. "Pang had the motive! The means! The opportunity!"

The chief inspector let that sink in.

Then he made one last forceful point: "But now, gentlemen, the opportunity is *ours*—and I should say we have the motive and means, as well, from a law enforcement standpoint. Because Dr. Pang is in France for the Presidential Ball this very night! And it is there that we will arrest him . . . for the murder of Yves Gluant, and the theft of the Pink Panther!"

He dropped his head in a curt bow, and the investigators began to applaud, the sound ringing through the high-ceilinged office like a twenty-one-gun salute. Soon the experts were on their feet, and the chief inspector stood with his chin high, basking in the adulation of his peers.

Renard, however, had just received word of a

late-breaking development in the case, and he rushed to Dreyfus's side.

Cupping a hand to whisper in his superior's ear, Renard said, "Chief Inspector—Clouseau has returned to France . . ."

Dreyfus scowled. "But we thought he would be kept busy in America for days!"

"He kept busy, all right. He was arrested by our own men upon his arrival back in the country!"

Dreyfus's eyes popped. "Arrested?" He suppressed a giggle, and asked, "On what charge?"

"Terrorism! The details are sketchy, but apparently there was a fuss on the plane coming over, and talk of an explosion."

His eye was not twitching, but his lips were, with barely contained glee, as he said, "Oh my dear, what a terrible tragedy. Whatever could have happened?"

It had begun with a small incident, at JFK Airport, at the security checkpoint.

While the lovely Xania had been treated like royalty—the guards beaming at her fawningly as they sent her fancy deco purse and other carry-ons through the X-ray apparatus—Clouseau had been singled out for a "routine search."

Standing in his shorts and t-shirt and socks and shoes, Clouseau said, "I see nothing 'routine' about the rubber glove! . . . What is your name, sir! I, Inspector Jacques Clouseau, will report you to the highest French authorities!"

The smug security guard said, "My name's Terry, sir."

" 'Terry.' Is this your only name? Surely you have more than one."

"Sure. Ahki."

"I will make the formal complaint, Monsieur Terry Ahki! Ponton!"

Clouseau's partner, in line nearby, stepped up to them. "Yes, Inspector?"

"Use my little digital camera there, and take a picture of me with this insubordinate Ahki fellow . . . Uh, no. Not from that position, from . . . yes, from right there! That is the best angle . . ."

In fact the angle from which Ponton took the picture also caught Xania in the background, as she and her things went through security.

On the way over, they had flown Air France, and because of Clouseau's celebrity as the "Pink Panther Detective" and the captor of the Gas-Mask Bandits, he and Ponton had been upgraded to first-class tickets. In rearranging his flight home, to take the same one as Xania, Clouseau had had to put up with yet another American insult, with Ponton deposited in the second cabin and the inspector dragged to the rear of the plane, where apparently children, animals and lepers were consigned.

The menu, however, in a cabin that seemed to

be third class (or perhaps thirteenth), Clouseau was pleased to find included a number of appetizing selections. He chose the sushi.

"Sauce?" the attractive female flight attendant asked.

"Yes, I would not object to some liquid of the alcoholic persuasion."

"No, the drink cart comes later . . . I mean, on your sushi. Do you want teriyaki?"

Clouseau's eyes narrowed. "Then you saw the indignities to which I was subjected!"

"Pardon?"

"I do indeed 'want' Terry Ahki—and I will *have* Terry Ahki!"

The stewardess made a face. "Whatever you say . . ."

When the sushi came out of the galley up front, it was perfectly fine. But along the interminable journey to the back of the plane, the food seemed to deteriorate, even to change color, the rice suddenly appearing rather moldy. It did not help that several people with colds and flu sneezed on Clouseau's order.

The inspector, who had skipped breakfast, did not notice the less-than-fresh appearance of the sushi. He merely popped one after another into his mouth, enjoying the succulent fishy flavor. The sauce was excellent, too—he wondered what it was called.

The trip to the "Apple Beeg" had been whirl-wind, and Clouseau being only human, it began to catch up with him. He slept in his uncomfort-able seat, his stomach full and warm as the amoe-bas swam and multiplied, and as the minutes passed, his belly moved and pulsed and throbbed, as if an alien were about to burst out.

The rumbling in his belly finally woke him, his eyes so wide that the white showed all around. He glanced down at his churning stomach.

The trouble down below! he thought.

Stuck at the rear of the plane, however, he was at least close to the restrooms in his cabin. Unfor-tunately, both bore OUT OF ORDER signs.

Thankfully the aisle was clear.

He ran to the next restroom, encountering a line of seven, and the next, where a maintenance man was making a repair, and the next—OCCUPADO!

Finally he was all the way forward in the first-class cabin, and the bathroom was free . . . and available! With a sigh of relief, he began to open the door, but the hand of a flight attendant landed lightly on his arm.

With a glazed smile and eyes colder than Hitler, the female flight attendant said, "Sir, this restroom is for first-class passengers only. You'll have to go back to your own cabin."

"But I suffer the stomach poisoning, from your vile airline food! It is the emergency *extreme*!"

"Sir, I am sorry. It's impossible. Go back to your cabin, and use—"

His expression hysterical, Clouseau gripped the startled woman by the arms. "You do not understand, mademoiselle! I will go off like the *buemb* if you do not allow me passage!"

"Buemb?" the flight attendant asked. "You mean . . . *bomb?*"

"Yes, the buemb! *I will explode!* Do you hear me—*explode!*"

That was when the five air marshals—flying in first class, in plainclothes, one in woman's attire, yanking off "her" wig—jumped the inspector.

On the plus side, Clouseau shortly no longer had the stomach problem, and soon was given a nice fresh orange jumpsuit to take the place of his own, slightly soiled suit.

From his office balcony, the chief inspector—his faithful deputy at his side—watched the startling procession below as a police van arrived at the Palais de la Justice parking lot to transfer the prisoner, Jacques Clouseau, to the phalanx of waiting officers.

"So much," Dreyfus said with a nasty little smile, his eye tic a memory now, "for the heroic 'Pink Panther Detective' . . ."

Clouseau, in bright orange prisoner garb, was dragged unceremoniously along, his hands cuffed behind him, and—with his partner, Ponton, walking freely behind—brought around to the front of the building.

Renard said, "Why not the prisoner's entrance at the rear, Chief Inspector?"

"For a public figure like Clouseau? No, no, my dear, Renard—he deserves public display."

Public disgrace, you mean, Renard thought, but said nothing.

"Take me to him," Dreyfus said. "This is one interrogation I will conduct . . . personally."

In the same interrogation booth, where not long ago Clouseau had grilled suspects himself, sat Clouseau—himself a suspect.

While Ponton and Renard looked on, Dreyfus—hands clasped behind him—circled the confused prisoner.

"So," the chief inspector said. "I entrust to you the greatest case of the new century, I allow you to traipse across the ocean to seek a suspect, and you repay my trust, my confidence, with terrorist activity? Explain yourself."

Clouseau shrugged. "It began, I suppose, with my father reading to me the Sherlock Holmes—"

"No, you nincompoop! *What* was going to explode?"

"Nothing—I had no buemb."

"Buemb?"

"Buemb! Buemb! I *had* no *buemb!*"

"Then *what* was going to explode?"

Clouseau blanched. He had his dignity. How could he tell the chief inspector of the Police Nationale that he had had the revenge of Montezuma, the trots explosive?

Head held high, Clouseau said, "I do not choose to tell you."

"Is that right?"

"If a man does not have his dignity, he has nothing."

"And who said that?"

Clouseau glanced behind him, then returned his gaze to the chief inspector. "Well, I have said that. Just now. You were here. Weren't you listening?"

Dreyfus, teeth bared, leaned in. "Listen to this, and listen carefully—on our force we have a complete idiot by the name of Clouseau, an inspector. He will be stripped of his rank, while I . . . the chief inspector of the Police Nationale . . . will personally take over his case!"

Clouseau's eyes narrowed. "It is odd that you would have a second Clouseau who is also an inspector. This is a coincidence strange . . ."

"You . . . you . . ." Even in this moment of triumph, Dreyfus was sputtering, and his tic had returned. ". . . you are a major incompetent!"

Sitting forward with a smile, Clouseau said, "Well, I hardly expected a promotion. This is a rank of which I am unfamiliar . . . the Major In-*comp*-et-an'. Will I report directly to you, Chief Inspector?"

Dreyfus's face was a mask of rage as he shouted, "Everyone——out!"

Clouseau began to rise.

"Not you!" Dreyfus said, and shoved him back into the chair. "Everyone get out while I have a . . . private moment with my 'star' detective . . ."

As directed, Ponton and Renard slipped out; but what Dreyfus did not realize was that they then stepped into the adjacent observation booth behind two-way glass, and heard all of what followed.

Dreyfus again circled the prisoner. Then he planted himself before Clouseau and his lip drew back over his teeth in an expression of extreme contempt. "Understand something, you simpering fool—when I made you an inspector, when I put you in charge of so important an investigation, it was not because I thought you had *merit* . . . that your 'good' work in Fromage, and every other small town that got rid of you as soon as possible, had convinced me of your *value*. No. I chose you to be the front behind which I could conduct a *real* investigation, while the press followed you on one stupid wild goose chase after another. I wanted someone who would quietly get nowhere until I was ready to take over the case, personally and publicly!"

Clouseau, trying to follow this, said nothing.

"I picked you, because you were the most stupid policeman in France—the biggest, most complete idiot this, or any country, has ever seen."

Chin up, Clouseau said, "I am a detective. An investigator . . ."

"You are a fool. A clown. A joke."

Clouseau's eyes tensed, but his mouth was slack. "Fool? Clown? Joke?"

"Yes, a poor hopeless deluded idiot."

"And I was not promoted for my merits?"

"Name one *single* merit! Were you listening to me, you boob? Even your partner was working for me, watching your every moronic move and reporting back."

"My partner . . . ? Ponton . . . ?"

Behind the glass, Ponton's head fell. Renard looked at him with sympathy and placed a supportive hand on the big man's shoulder.

"Clouseau, the only problem in my thinking was that I did not anticipate that you would bring to France a reign of terror that would make the French Revolution look like a house party at a nunnery."

". . . My charm?"

Dreyfus blinked. "What?"

Clouseau smiled weakly. "You asked me to name one of my merits. I put forward my charm as a—"

"You can't even conduct a normal *conversation!*"

Clouseau swallowed, straightened. "I do have my merits, and my methods. I have been pursuing a killer, and a thief. And I beg you to allow me to complete my inquiries so that I may—"

"You spent all of your time trying to make yourself look like a *hero*, you ridiculous cretin! Well, now you will be stripped of your rank, ridiculed in the media, and I? I will be *done* with you!"

Clouseau stared with puppy-dog eyes at the inspector. "I thought we were friends . . . colleagues. With the respect mutual . . ."

"Well you were, as usual, dead wrong, weren't you, Clouseau? . . . Now if you will excuse me, I have to prepare to make an arrest that will clinch for me the Medal of Honor, and possibly catapult me to the National Assembly. Let me not say *au revoir*, Clouseau, rather—good riddance."

In the hallway, as Dreyfus exited the interrogation booth, Renard asked, "Shall we lock him up?"

"No. He is finished. I don't know what happened on that plane, but Clouseau is only a 'terrorist' by accident. Start the papers for his early retirement, and let him go home to his obscurity."

Ponton took the wheel of the Renault and drove the devastated Clouseau—who had said nothing since the interrogation had ended—to his apartment building.

Ponton parked, and as Clouseau got out so did the bigger man, coming around and offering his hand.

"I apologize to you," Ponton said, "and hope you will still consider me your partner."

Clouseau smiled a little and shook the man's hand, but said, "I am afraid there will be no more partners for Clouseau, my large associate."

"Please believe that I did not know to what extent the chief inspector was using you—I knew only that he wanted reports on your activities . . . and I came to understand that he had a certain . . ."

"Contempt for Clouseau?"

Ponton sighed and nodded.

"You are a fine man, Ponton," Clouseau said, with surprising dignity. "I am the fool. You were the teacher, and I the pupil. If ever I made you to look the fool, my friend . . . I am sorry."

"Don't be silly. I feel we were making progress. I think we would have cracked this case—soon."

Clouseau said, "I felt this way myself . . . before learning that I was the idiot deluded."

Ponton waved that off. "Don't listen to that megalomaniac Dreyfus! He is all ambition and no heart—that way lies madness. The day will come when he will pay."

"That day, my friend, is not this day."

"Perhaps not." Ponton rose to his full height and saluted Clouseau. "But it was nonetheless an honor serving under you, sir."

Clouseau returned the salute, then lowered it in a bladed karate chop . . . which landed, soft as a feather, gentle as a kiss, on Ponton's chest.

And Clouseau turned and—perhaps the most

dejected man on the planet, but certainly in France—walked into his apartment building.

When the late afternoon news came on, Clouseau was in his flat sitting on the sofa before his television. Having adjusted the rabbit-ear antenna, he watched fatalistically as footage of himself being dragged into the Palais de la Justice consumed the screen.

Then the man who Clouseau had thought was his superior, but was in fact his nemesis, was interviewed in a press conference.

Confident, smiling, Chief Inspector Charles Dreyfus fielded all questions, after a brief statement announcing that he was personally taking over the Pink Panther investigation . . . and that an arrest was "imminent."

A television reporter called out, "Sir, the coroner has announced that Bizu was killed by a perfect shot in the occipital lobe. Any comment?"

"While no detail is unimportant, this one does not seem to have any particular significance."

But Clouseau was sitting up, thinking that over. Aloud he muttered, "The lobe occipital . . . the lobe occipital . . . He is wrong. That is important. That is *most* important . . ."

When the interview was over, Clouseau clicked off the TV and, still thinking, went to his little digital camera, which lay on the desk nearby. A relatively new purchase, the camera came with a small instruction booklet which Clouseau had carefully filed in a drawer, where he found it now.

With surprising ease Clouseau followed the instructions. When unconcerned with his public dignity, he could accomplish any number of tasks. Soon the digital camera's little screen was showing him the various pictures he'd taken in New York. Some of them featured himself and/or Ponton, having a great time there; but then came shots of Clouseau being frisked and abused by that "swine security guard" at the airport.

"I will *still* report this outrage," he said out loud. "This Terrance Ahki will receive the reprimand severe . . ."

As he studied the photo, he noticed—in the background of the picture—Xania was moving through security, specifically undergoing the X-ray of her carry-on items.

Sorrowfully he thought, *Ah, but will you still love me, my curvaceous little songbird, after Clouseau has suffered the indignity publique?*

Then he recalled why he had been so specific about where Ponton should stand while taking the picture; his detective's instincts had told him that having a record of what that X-ray machine had seen might prove worthwhile . . .

He looked closer at the photo. In the little screen, the image was too small to truly reveal what Clouseau thought he saw, so he returned to the camera's instruction booklet.

Reading aloud, Clouseau said, " 'How to Enlarge a Photo . . .' "

And within minutes he was on the phone, catching Ponton just as the detective was getting home.

"My conspicuous confrere, I must ask you to come over here, immediately! Redemption, she wriggles her seductive nose at Clouseau!"

"I am on my way."

His next call was to Nicole, at the chief inspector's office.

"My little spectacled confection, are you going to the Presidential Ball tonight?"

"Why, yes . . . alone."

"I beg to differ. You will attend with Clouseau, the former inspector."

"That's lovely . . . But are you sure you're up to it?"

"Yes, I have had my prescription refilled . . . Oh, I mean, I will meet you there . . . but first go to my office and bring me my vinyl bag with the marking, 'Presidential Palace.' It is in the bottom drawer, filed under 'P.' You will see it quickly because it is the only vinyl bag filed there."

"Of course, but . . . why?"

"Because it is time that the case, she be solved."

"But, Jacques . . . aren't you off the force?"

"Not yet. Not quite yet. The tape that is red has yet to be snipped. And while I may be no longer officially the inspector . . . I am still the officer of the leau."

"Of the what?"

"Hurry! I will see you there . . ."

THIRTEEN

Return of the Pink Panther

Within the grand palace of the President, preparations for the ball were in their final, fevered minutes, security staff, delivery men and caterers hustling, bustling, each on a mission of extreme importance.

No mission was more important, Chief Inspector Charles Dreyfus knew, than his own: to unmask a murderer and thief, at the most high-profile event of the year.

Resplendent in his tuxedo, the chief inspector—checking over the guest list at the door, with the evening's head of security—crossed off a key name: Inspector Jacques Clouseau.

"This should have been removed earlier," he

said sternly. "After his public humiliation, it would be most embarrassing for all concerned for this buffoon to be allowed into an affair of state such as this."

"I apologize for the oversight." The security chief leaned in confidentially. "We do have one problem, sir."

"Yes?"

"We've had more requests from the press than anticipated. There is a rumor afloat that the Pink Panther case will be resolved tonight, at the ball itself—how this rumor began, and managed to spread, who can say?"

"It is a mystery," Dreyfus said with a tiny smile.

"But we'll have many media persons here who are *not* on our approved list. What shall I do?"

Dreyfus gestured with a grand hand. "Check their credentials, and allow them in—we value a free press in France."

The security chief frowned doubtfully. "We can't let them attend the *party* . . ."

"No, but you *can* corral them somewhere, until I tell you that the time is right."

"Certainly, sir."

Then let them pour in, Dreyfus thought, *to see my moment of triumph* . . .

Clouseau directed Ponton to drive, the big man opening up the little convertible in a way its owner had never attempted. The acceleration threw Clouseau backward, and—for a time—he flapped in the wind like a flag as the little car raced for the Presidential Palace; passing along the Seine, the "flag" swinging out over the river-banks, the former inspector's change rained from his pockets onto several sunbathing beauties, who perhaps thought he was complimenting them with a tip.

Nonetheless, he managed to climb back into the vehicle and fill in his partner on his new theories, based upon the recent evidence he had uncovered, and pieced together . . .

"Gluant and Bizu were killed by the same person, my Promethean protege . . . and that killer intends to strike again tonight!"

"But, Inspector—"

Clouseau raised a hand. "While I am no longer the inspector, I will allow you to call me such, as I intend to regain that rank this evening. You no doubt wonder why the modus operandi differs between the murders . . ."

"Yes! Bizu killed by a rifle, Gluant by a poisoned Chinese dart . . ."

Clouseau shrugged. "Sometimes I like the vichyssoise, other times I like the potato soup!"

"But . . . Inspector . . . vichyssoise *is* potato soup."

"You are wrong, Ponton! One, she is hot . . . the other, she is very cold . . . The murder of Gluant was motivated by hatred, and that of Bizu in the cold blood of the practical instinct of survival by this killer."

"I don't understand, Inspector."

"Understand this—this killer means to confuse. To make us think that perhaps these murderers were the work of two perpetrators . . . but there is only one."

"You are sure of this?"

"As sure as I am that the question is not, 'How were these two murders different?' but 'What did these dead men have in common?' "

As the little car blurred through the city, Ponton took his eyes off the road to look at his partner. "We both know what they had in common—your precious pop star."

"The lovely Xania. Precisely."

"Then . . . *she* killed them?"

"No, Ponton . . ." Clouseau turned his gaze upon the larger man. His words were heavy with melodramatic meaning. ". . . She is the next *victim!*"

When they arrived at the palace, at first things went well; their little car, despite a presence among Rolls Royces and Mercedes, received the respectful attention of valets. At the top of the stairs at the front door, the attractive female ticket taker smiled pleasantly and checked for their names on her list.

Names that weren't there.

What *was* there were burly security men blocking the way, thugs in tuxedos. Clouseau knew his burly associate might well take on these goons, and successfully; but such a conspicuous entry would only be met by an army of such brutes, whose strength in numbers would defeat even the likes of Ponton.

As Clouseau and his assistant walked down the stairs, intending to regroup and come up with a Plan B, a birdcall trilled from nearby bushes. Clouseau glanced toward the shrubbery and saw the glint of eyeglasses.

Nicole.

They rushed around behind to meet her, and found a radiant vision in a formal gown. But her stunningly low-cut ensemble included an unlikely accessory: a large, rather bulky vinyl bag. She looked like a prom queen about to elope.

She also had something rolled up under an arm: blueprints!

"Inspector," she said breathlessly, "is this what you wanted?"

She hefted the bag.

"It is," Clouseau said, beaming at her. "It is indeed."

"And I thought you might need these . . ." She thrust forward the rolled-up prints. ". . . the architectural plans of the palace . . ."

Clouseau opened the large, scroll-like documents and murmured appreciatively, "Good work, my dear . . . good work."

Ponton took the bag from Nicole, and asked his partner, "And what is this?"

His old confidence back, Clouseau said, "It is camouflage fashioned for me especially by my good friend Monsieur Balls, the master of the disguise."

Chuckling, shaking his head, Ponton said, "You never fail to surprise me, Inspector."

With a wicked laugh, Clouseau said, "With me, my friend, the surprises, they are never unexpected." He turned to the stunning young secretary. "Wish us luck, Nicole. Or as they say in the business of show, break the leg."

She gazed at him admiringly, touching his arm. "You don't need luck to break the leg—you are Inspector Clouseau."

"Not," he said, "anymore . . . but I will be again—soon! Thanks to the two of you, my charming accomplices. And as for you, my pet . . ."

He moved closer to the lovely Nicole. He put his hands on either side of her sweet face, then lifted off her glasses, saying, "As in the old film, I have the feeling you would be even more beautiful without these . . . Ah yes! I was right."

In the moonlight, in the garden of the Presidential Palace, there had surely never been a more beautiful woman than Nicole. She lifted her lips to Clouseau's, and Ponton looked away discreetly as she and the inspector shared a sweet kiss.

Then, her glasses in one hand, Nicole slipped

away, followed by the sound of her tripping and falling into the bushes.

"My dear!" Clouseau called discreetly. "Perhaps, for just tonight . . . put the glasses back on?"

The Presidential Ball was in full sway; dignitaries both French and foreign, honored guests and celebrities from all over Europe and America as well, danced and dined and chatted and laughed. Under the artificial starlight of glittering chandeliers, with a full orchestra providing a soundtrack and waiters carrying trays of champagne-filled glasses in a never-ending procession, few of the distinguished and celebrated attendees in their tuxedos, gowns, and jewelry could ever have guessed that on this sparkling night the crime of the new century would be solved.

At the top of the list of the handful in the know was Chief Inspector Charles Dreyfus, who had seen to it that every major suspect in the Pink Panther case was present. From Rome had come the casino owner Larocque, like a high-priced undertaker in his black tux, attended by his mysterious Asian bodyguard; and the singing sensation Xania had been invited to perform, a clever way to "honor" her while making sure her presence as a suspect was fulfilled.

Team France was represented by their lovely PR person, Cherie Dubois; the new coach Vainqueur; and the handsome star, blond Jacquard.

Interestingly, the Minister of Justice had brought his mistress tonight, a widow high in social circles, a lovely lady who wore a pink diamond ring—impressive, but no Pink Panther. There they stood, in front of God and everyone, making cocktail conversation with the President himself. Was Clochard, a divorcé, thinking of making his latest love an honest woman, with this public appearance?

But the real focus of Dreyfus's attention (and that of his undercover men, spread throughout the ballroom) was Dr. Li How Pang—in white evening wear, knocking back drink after drink, the Chinese Minister of Sport setting a very lax example for the athletes of the world. Was the good doctor nervous, being so close to the chief inspector who was closing in on him? Or was the man merely a lush?

And when the moment for the great arrest came, there would be no escape for Dr. Pang. Dreyfus knew the layout of the ballroom, the palace itself, as intimately as that of his own house: at either end of the vast, elegant room were staircases with balconies; large central windows at left looked out upon lushly landscaped grounds—high enough from the floor to make egress improbable, with wide, floor-length plush floral-patterned curtains on either side, a stretch of finely veined marble wall between the plumes of curtain. Opposite the windows was the stage, where the orchestra played and, soon, Xania would entertain.

The hard-eyed, no-nonsense head of security approached Dreyfus cautiously. "Sir," he said quietly, "my people report having seen Inspector Clouseau and his ex-partner, Ponton, on the grounds this evening."

"Forget Ponton," Dreyfus said. "As for Clouseau, he may be trying to make a last-ditch, grandstand play at nabbing the killer himself."

"What should we do with him?"

"The fool is trespassing—arrest him, of course."

"Certainly, Chief Inspector. Discreetly."

"Oh, no! Drag him in, in handcuffs right through here, parade the fool in front of the party. He is a rogue officer, and he must be taught."

"Yes, Chief Inspector."

"Clouseau's capture is a priority second only to that of the murderer himself."

The security chief nodded curtly, then whispered into his lapel microphone, and soon all of the security people were on alert.

Renard stepped up beside his superior. "All is well, I trust?"

"Yes—Dr. Pang is here, tossing down cocktails, feeling no pain."

"I trust Pang will feel pain soon enough."

"Oh yes, Renard. Oh yes . . . In just about ten minutes . . ."

* * *

In a dressing room as elegant and lavishly outfitted as the finest boudoir, Xania—in her form-fitting, low-cut sleeveless gown—sat at an art deco make-up mirror that dated back at least as far as her ever-present Josephine Baker clutch purse, putting the finishing touches on her flawless face.

Uninvited, unannounced, Raymond Larocque —accompanied by Huang, his hulking Asian bodyguard, who looked like a genie in a tuxedo— stepped into the dressing room and approached the mirror.

Looking at her in the glass, leaning in over her shoulder, Larocque smiled his snake's smile and said, "Mirror, mirror . . . who's the loveliest of all? Why, Xania, of course . . ."

She glared back defiantly at his reflection. "I guess a wicked witch like you would know."

"Hmmmm. Trifle bitchy tonight, aren't we? You're just nervous with all these police here, all this security."

"And why would that make me nervous?"

A smile twitched, though the eyes in the handsome face were dark hard stones, unblinking in their gaze. "Because, my sweet . . . I *know* you killed Yves."

She huffed, and touched a powder-puff to a perfect nose. "You know no such thing. If you're trying to intimidate me, you are as pathetic as that overgrown chaperone of yours."

She sneered at Huang in the mirror, and he gave her a pouty look, and turned away.

Larocque put a hand on her bare shoulder. "Don't misunderstand me . . . I couldn't care less if you killed Yves Gluant a thousand times. I would have rather he suffered, frankly, but I will settle for dead."

She removed that cold hand from her flesh. "This is a private dressing room. You and your date, get out of here."

Ignoring that, Larocque cast a gaze that held hers as he said, "All I care about is that ring . . . the Pink Panther. *It belongs to me.*"

Her lips were firm as she said, "First of all, I don't have the stupid goddamn thing. Second, why in hell would it belong to *you*, anyway?"

The casino owner straightened, folded his arms, but his eyes were still locked with hers in the mirror. "I think you know the reasons . . . the debt your late lover owed me. But that's not important."

"Oh? What is it?"

"That I *want* it. That I want to possess the Pink Panther, much as so many men look at you and want to possess your flesh and the nicely rounded package it protects. But what they don't understand, such men, is how fleeting beauty can be. I am a collector—I desire beauty of permanence."

Her eyes shot icicles at him, but she said nothing.

His fingers caressed her cheek—his touch had been cold before; now it was hot.

"Yes, beauty *can* be fleeting, don't you think? A splash of acid, the flick of a blade . . . How sad it would be for ugly things to happen to such a very pretty girl . . ."

When Larocque and Huang had left her alone in the dressing room, Xania looked at herself in the mirror, at the features that had combined with her talent to put her at the top of the entertainment game.

Then she buried her face in her hands and wept.

When she was done, she cleansed her face and again, methodically, coolly, began to reapply her make-up.

Before long, the lights dimmed, and the audience turned toward the stage, where they could see the silhouette of a lovely woman, applying lipstick . . .

Then the lights came up and Xania turned and smiled at them, as if she'd been caught in a private moment, and tucked her lipstick tube in the ever-present purse, which she lay on the piano nearby, moving toward the microphone.

She began with one of her hits, an upbeat number with techno touches, at once retro and yet very twenty-first century. Even the older dignitaries among the distinguished crowd were impressed by her beauty, confidence and obvious talent, as she wove a spell both melodic and rhythmic.

Not all eyes were on the beauty onstage, however—Dreyfus's security team did their best to visually roam the crowd and the periphery, their view especially on any possible entrance or exit.

But in lighting that had gone subdued in honor of the entertainer onstage, the guards missed a subtle movement toward the top of those floral curtains beside the wide expanse of windows. Had the lights been up full, security might have seen Clouseau—in one of his best disguises, face forward, arms spread as if Leonardo da Vinci had drawn him—camouflaged against the curtains in a unitard of the exact same floral pattern. Near him a larger lump in the curtain proved to be Ponton, similarly attired.

The two detectives, on their backs, managed to move clingingly along the curtains until that expanse of marble above the windows, at which point they flipped over and revealed the opposite side of their unitards, which perfectly matched the color and veined-marble pattern of the wall, fingertips hugging a lip along the top.

The only one in the room who noticed these flies on the wall was Nicole—her glasses on again—and she alone knew what they were up to. When she spotted Dreyfus regarding her with narrowed eyes, she returned her attention to the stage, and moved nearer to her boss, looping an arm through his and commenting on how wonderful Xania was.

Dreyfus, eyes still tight, mouth open, nodded numbly, then glanced toward the windows where he saw nothing. He next cast his gaze at Dr. Pang, who was wandering from his position in the crowd back to one of the several bars.

Dreyfus spoke into his lapel mike. "Under no circumstances lose Pang . . . I want him under surveillance every second!"

Then, with a sigh, the chief inspector returned his attention to the stage. This Xania was a pleasant enough performer, but he really did not enjoy seeing anyone but himself in the spotlight.

Flipping back into the floral pattern, the precarious pair made it across the second set of curtains, then became marble again and soon slipped from above and swung down in an open door, unseen by guards standing nearby, their backs to these human insects.

"This wardrobe man of yours," Ponton whispered, "he is a genius."

He and Clouseau were at the bottom of a dark stairwell, getting out of their unitards.

"There is only one Balls," Clouseau admitted

to Ponton, now outfitted in similarly tight-fitting black catsuits like those the Gas-Mask Bandits had worn, covering all but the eyes of the wearer.

"What is the rest of the plan?" Ponton asked, his voice still hushed.

"There will be an attempt on Xania's life," Clouseau said, "but it will not be from the audience—the chief inspector has his security men too well placed for that."

"You suspect the assassin will strike from elsewhere?"

"Yes—studying the plans of the building, only the roof makes sense, and . . . what is *that*, my friend? Footsteps?"

And it was indeed footsteps, above them.

"I see him!" Ponton said, leaning out to look up. "He is all in black!"

"The bad ones, they always wear the black," Clouseau said, and the two men—in black—took pursuit.

Coincidences do happen.

And one of them happened that night, although perhaps it was an instance of great minds thinking alike; or at least, *minds* thinking alike . . .

For just as Clouseau had thought that to mimic the apparel of the Gas-Mask Bandits would be useful, providing a distracting and confusing element to the proceedings, so too had calculated the killer stalking Xania.

He, also, wore a black skintight catsuit that revealed only his eyes. And he, as well, had made himself familiar with the plans of the Presidential Palace. There the similarities between killer and detective ended.

For under the killer's arm was tucked a weapon, zipped away in a protective pouch—no ordinary weapon, either; it would kill quickly, and silently, and for a while, when the singer collapsed onstage, confusion would reign. Unlike a gunshot, exactly what had happened—and from whence death had emanated—would not immediately be apparent . . . long enough for him to slip away . . .

Right now, courtesy of those blueprints, the killer was taking the route that led him to just the right window, easily reached by stepping up onto a chair, which would give him access to the roof. Within moments, he was standing on the roof of the palace, under a sky flung with stars, in a breeze as soothing as the thought of life without those bastards Yves Gluant and Bizu, or (soon) that bitch Xania . . .

He padded across the roof toward the prominent jut of the skylight. According to the building plans, the skylight should provide a window with an overview of the ballroom, and a decent angle on the stage. He stopped and, almost prayerfully, knelt at what should be the right spot . . .

And was.

He had the perfect view of Xania, who was singing her heart out even as she provided an equally perfect target.

He removed from the zippered pouch his weapon—a crossbow. He loaded it. The projectile that would strike Xania in the throat, however, was no arrow—nothing so unsophisticated would do. This was a bullet of sorts, albeit notched and feathered, nothing to stick out of the dead woman's neck to point back at him.

She should be grateful, this nasty bitch—she would be a legend, thanks to him! Her record sales would skyrocket. She would be richer than she had ever dreamed, swimming in money . . .

Just a little too dead to spend any of it . . .

Clouseau and Ponton were not doing as well.

The masks kept slipping down over their eyes, and when Clouseau wasn't bumping into furniture, Ponton was bumping into him. They had taken the stairway to a hall, and they had lost their prey—no footsteps, no man in black, nothing but each other.

"Did you see where he went?" Ponton asked, out of breath.

"No. I must have Balls write the manufacturer of this outfit and complain about this swine mask."

"I don't know—looks kind of spiffy on you, Inspector."

Beneath the mask, Clouseau beamed. "Well, thank you, Ponton, I—"

"Inspector—*look!* It is ajar!"

Clouseau moved the mask into place and followed Ponton's pointing finger to the gaping window above the chair. "No, my unobservant friend, that is not a jar. It is a window . . . but more significantly, it is open!"

Nodding, Ponton said, "Those building plans indicate that window leads out to a half-roof, and from there—"

Clouseau's eyes flared. "The skylight!"

As they moved toward the window, they had a view on the skylight above, and could see another window, more than ajar: *open* . . . and through it pointed downward the snout of a crossbow.

Clouseau clutched Ponton by the arm. "While it is true that there are perhaps a million of the explanation why a crossbow might be harmlessly pointing down into a room of party guests, we must not take the chance! To the roof!"

Ponton helped Clouseau through the window, and—for once—no mishaps ensued; within moments they were on the roof, and could see the kneeling figure in black, his finger wrapped around the crossbow trigger.

The two detectives ran across the rooftop, and the killer, seeing them, got to his feet, ditched his weapon, and ran.

"Goddamn you lousy cops!" the killer blurted in English.

Master of languages that he was, Clouseau called out, on the run, "The zheeg, she is urrp!"

The killer had no idea that Clouseau had just told him "the jig is up," but did not linger for discussion. Using his knowledge of the building's layout, the killer leapt down onto a lower level of rooftop, to slip back inside through another window.

And one man in black was pursued by two others.

Unaware that the former Inspector Clouseau and his ex-partner, Detective Second Class Gilbert Ponton, were chasing an assassin through the corridors of the Presidential Palace, Chief Inspector Charles Dreyfus was about to make his move.

He had already signaled his men to encircle Dr. Pang.

Xania's performance had ended, and she was taking a bow to enthusiastic applause from the sophisticated audience.

Dreyfus whispered to his security chief, via lapel mike, "Time to let in the Fourth Estate."

Patiently the chief inspector waited for several minutes until he noted the media streaming in through virtually every door, cameras and microphones at the ready.

Into his lapel mike, Dreyfus snapped, *"Now!"*

Suddenly China's Minister of Sport—his latest cocktail in hand—stood with shocked eyes, swivelling as he realized men all around were bearing in, pointing handguns right at him.

The ripple of excitement and, yes, fear that moved through the crowd only pleased Dreyfus. This night, this *moment*, was one these self-important VIPs would never forget.

Like the Red Sea opening for the Chosen People, the crowd parted for Chief Inspector Charles Dreyfus as he walked slowly, deliberately toward the Chinese dignitary, who stood frozen, too disconcerted to be indignant.

Or perhaps . . . too guilty.

"Allow me to welcome you to tonight's festivities, Dr. Pang," Dreyfus said. "I represent the government of France, specifically the Police Nationale. I welcome you even though you have insulted us, coming here to make a mockery of our country and her officials."

Now Dr. Pang's eyes drew tight and he said, "How dare you! Who do you think you are, making—"

"I am Chief Inspector Charles Dreyfus . . . and I am here to arrest *you*, Dr. Pang, in the name of the great nation of France, for the murder of Yves Gluant!"

Another wave of excitement rolled across the assemblage, and flashbulbs popped and strobed as if a small fireworks display had been set off to honor the great detective who had solved France's most important mystery.

But another commotion trumped Dreyfus's moment.

A clatter on the landing of the stairway at left turned every eye in the room onto three men in black—one on the run, two in hot pursuit.

Ooohs and *aaahs* ensued as a scene of action straight out of the cinema played out before the astonished eyes of the partygoers.

The man in the lead leapt onto the endless bannister and began to slide expertly down. The nearest pursuer followed suit, and he too began a gliding ride.

Dreyfus stepped forward, thrust a finger toward the melee, and turned purple as he shouted to Renard, "One of them must be Clouseau! Arrest him at once!"

Renard, confounded by this, shrugged with open hands. "But *which* is Clouseau?"

The third man in black leapt onto the bannister and promptly fell off, tumbling over the ledge.

"*That* would be Clouseau," Dreyfus said.

But just as Clouseau had tumbled over the ledge, the man in the lead—the killer—nimbly alighted from the bannister and began to round the corner, toward a nearby door. The killer did not count on Jacques Clouseau, however; or at least, did not count on Jacques Clouseau falling directly on him, and flattening him like a squashed boog.

Bug.

Clouseau leapt to his feet. "In the name of the statutes and laws of the great nation of France, I arrest you for the murder of Yves Gluant!"

Other than the echo of Clouseau's voice, no sound could be heard in the great hall.

Then Clouseau ripped the mask from the killer's catsuit and revealed his features to the world.

"You are the killer," Clouseau declared. *"Yuri . . . the trainer who trains!"*

The newsmen whose cameras had been centered on Dreyfus and his suspect, Dr. Pang, had by now all swung around on the former inspector and *his* suspect.

Ponton hauled Yuri to his feet, but there were no denials from the killer.

In fact, he blurted a confession that was caught by half a dozen video cameras.

"Yves Gluant . . ." Yuri spat on the floor. ". . . he was *nothing!* A pretty face, a poster boy! It was *I* who drew up the plays, who designed Team France's brilliant offense! He takes credit for my genius! He takes this from me, and tells me I am lucky that he 'saved' me from Mother Russia. He treats me like a piece of meat! Now he *is* the piece of meat . . . the piece of dead meat."

Dreyfus stumbled forward. "But the poison was Chinese . . . ?"

Ponton said to Clouseau, "Yes, Inspector—why

did you suspect Yuri when the evidence pointed elsewhere?"

"The *wrong* evidence, she pointed elsewhere," Clouseau said. "The *right* evidence, she pointed to this man, to this moment. Think back? You were there, Ponton—when I interrogated the Chinese woman? She say to me, 'Why do you bother me, you fool? Just because I am Chinese, and this soccer player was killed with a Chinese poison? Why don't you question the soccer trainers—they are required to have knowledge of Chinese herbs!' "

Dreyfus was scowling in stunned disbelief. "I never heard of such a thing . . ."

"I know," Ponton said, dumbfounded. "He really *does* know Chinese . . ."

"The Yu woman was right," Clouseau said. "I looked it up myself—statute 87223 . . . every trainer of the national soccer team must have knowledge of the Chinese herbs."

His upper lip peeled back, Dreyfus blurted, "There's no such statute under French law!"

Clouseau waggled a gently lecturing finger. "Not under French law—in the rule and regulation of the French sporting code. This knowledge of the herb Chinese, it makes child's play for Yuri to fashion the poison dart, and kill this coach he despised, while sending the less experienced investigator on the chase for the wild Chinese goose."

From the crowd a reporter asked, "But, Inspector—who killed Bizu?"

Clouseau nodded toward the suspect, who was in Ponton's custody, hanging his head, dejection and hatred twisting his features.

"Again, the trainer who trains is also the killer who kills . . . Bizu had often heard of Yuri's hatred for his coach. Perhaps he lends the ear sympathetic, no? But then Bizu . . . his star position at risk, his days as the hero waning . . . takes advantage to blackmail Yuri. It is never wise to try to extort from the murderer the money—more often, you get only more murder."

Dreyfus stepped forward. "This is a ridiculous theory . . . Yuri is a trainer of athletes. But that shot was made by a master marksman!"

"Ah, Chief Inspector, you are learning," Clouseau said condescendingly. "Yes, it was a stunningly well-placed shot, burrowing deeply into the head . . . into the occipital lobe."

"Exactly." Dreyfus threw up his hands. "And this man is no expert marksman."

"Oh but now you are wrong, Chief Inspector— I refer you to Russian Army statute 611: all soldiers must be excellent marksmen trained to kill human targets with precision, specifically to know and understand the location of the occipital lobe."

Xania had come down from the stage, and now moved toward the front of the crowd. Her eyes went to the captive Yuri, and he snarled at her, "You bitch . . . you lucky *bitch!*"

Clouseau smiled, just a little. "Yes, Yuri, she was lucky that Clouseau and his able partner Ponton were there to save her life . . . because you hate her, do you not?"

The trainer's eyes were mad in all sense of the word. "More . . . more than *anything* . . ."

"You had helped her when she was a young struggling artist, and then she cast you aside, turned her back on you."

Dreyfus, rolling his eyes, blurted, "And how in the name of heaven could you know that, Clouseau?"

"I," Clouseau said with a suave nod toward the singer, "am a charter member of the Xania Fan Club. There was a mention of this in an article entitled, 'The Struggling Days,' in issue two, volume one, page seven, paragraph three . . . no, four."

Dreyfus groaned.

Clouseau whirled toward Yuri and thrust an accusing finger. "But you were one of the little people, eh? A five-foot-six-one, left behind when she turned to the strapping athlete, Bizu; and then to the hunk romantique who was Yves Gluant. *Another* reason you hated both men, no? . . . and the key reason why, tonight, from the high window, you attempted to kill this sweet young flower, who has tragically lost her virginity so many times."

Xania looked at the floor.

With a grand sigh, Clouseau turned to his audience, which included his chief inspector.

"And so at last," Clouseau said, "the case, it is solved."

From the front of the crowd came cries from a dozen reporters: *"But the diamond?" "The Pink Panther?" "What happened to the Pink Panther?"*

Dreyfus shushed the crowd, and said to Clouseau, "I thank you for allowing me to play a part in our mutual charade, Inspector."

Clouseau seemed confused, understandably so, for once. "But, Chief Inspector . . ."

To the audience, Dreyfus—with a sickly smile—explained, "I apologize to our honored guest, Dr. Pang, for making him a decoy in these proceedings. And I thank Inspector Clouseau for allowing me to stage the necessary farce of his 'disgrace' and demotion from rank."

The guests were looking at each other, shrugging, trying to follow this.

Dreyfus pressed on: "And I thank you, Inspector Clouseau, for diligently carrying out my instructions to the letter as you have."

Clouseau shrugged. "Certainly, Chief Inspector."

Now Dreyfus bore in on the trainer, still in Ponton's grasp. "And now the time has come—hand over that diamond, you swine!"

Quietly Clouseau agreed, "Yes, he is a swine. But not a thief."

Yuri snorted a humorless laugh. "What do I care of that filthy bauble? It holds no interest for me. I acted only for revenge . . . for justice . . . not for gain!"

"Chief Inspector," Clouseau said, tapping Dreyfus on the shoulder, prompting him to turn with a flummoxed expression. "Yuri, the trainer who trains? He does not have the diamond. Never has he had the diamond."

Dreyfus chuckled; there was no mirth in it. "But he's the murderer. He must have the diamond!"

"No. We have but one crime, here. Murder."

Dreyfus's eyes were golf balls. "Even for you, that is absurd, Clouseau! We're talking about the most famous theft of modern times! *Where is that stone?*"

His stride deliberate, Clouseau moved to Xania. He looked at her with fondness, and with sadness.

"There," he said.

And he pointed at the small clutch purse tucked under her arm.

The inspector explained: "In this purse . . . once owned by Josephine Baker . . . and Jerry Lewis . . ."

Clouseau waited several seconds for this largely French crowd to recover.

". . . she has tucked the precious Panther away, like the prize in the box Crackerjax."

Dreyfus strode over and snatched the small handbag away from the singer. Moving to a nearby table, he unceremoniously dumped out its contents; after sorting through make-up and other feminine trappings, Dreyfus shook his head.

"No," he said firmly. "Sorry, Clouseau . . . but no diamond."

"If I may, Chief Inspector?"

Clouseau casually walked over and took the purse. From his pocket came the trusty Swiss Army knife; he sliced open the lining of the purse, and poked in two fingers.

They returned with the Pink Panther, which Clouseau held to the light, where it glittered and sparkled and winked at every single person there.

The *ooohs* and *aaahs* from the crowd began as a panther-like purr and grew to almost a roar.

Then as Xania spoke, they hushed to pin-drop silence.

"Yes," she said. "I had it. But I did *not* steal it."

"Explain yourself!" Dreyfus demanded.

"That afternoon," she said, and her emotions were barely in control, "when Yves came to my box, at the front row in the stadium . . . he told me he still loved me. He said he was sorry for the terrible things he had done, and swore he would never cheat on me again . . . and he said he wanted me to marry him. He proved it by pressing the ring into my hands. It was our engagement ring, he said."

Clouseau stepped to her side and slipped a supporting arm around her shoulder. "If you examine those blow-up photos in your office, Chief Inspector, you will note that there is one that shows the coach missing the ring *before* the murder . . ."

Dreyfus said nothing.

Xania continued: "When Yves . . . Yves was murdered, how could I have come forward without the assumption being made that I had stolen the Panther? And yet the ring . . . because Yves had given it to me . . . meant very much to me, so much. I decided to keep it always, as a token of his love for me."

Dreyfus sneered. "Very sweet, I'm sure; but Gluant worked for the nation of France. In that light, I must now claim that ring for—"

"Uh, Chief Inspector, do forgive me," Clouseau said, "but according to civil statute 106, 'If a male citizen dies prior to marriage, his female intended has the right to retain ownership of any engagement ring, regardless of any associations said citizen might have to the state.' "

Dreyfus gaped at Clouseau with only slightly more hatred than Yuri's stare toward Xania.

"Xania, my lovely cleared suspect," Clouseau said, pressing the ring into her hand, "the Pink Panther, she is yours to keep."

THE PINK PANTHER

Ponton, still lugging Yuri, asked, "Inspector, how did you *know* Xania had the ring?"

"The photo you took of me at the airport, Ponton," Clouseau said with a gentle smile, "it captured the X-ray of the items carry-on of Xania. I merely blew the photo up on my small television screen, and, *voila*, there is the Pink Panther, in all her X-rayed glory! The security at the airport, they are looking for the gun, the knife, the buemb, not the missing diamond ring! . . . Chief Inspector, perhaps you would like a blow-up of that photo, for the collection in your office?"

Again, Dreyfus said nothing; he was staring, but at nothing in particular.

From the crowd came cries of *"Bravo!"* and *"Bravo, Clouseau!"* Even the jaded reporters shouted their adulation, and applause rang resoundingly through the great ballroom of the Presidential Palace.

Xania, with the most beautiful smile ever seen on the front page of a tabloid, hugged Clouseau and posed with him for the press, flashbulbs popping, strobing. The chant of *"Bravo, Clouseau"* built and echoed through the high-ceilinged chamber, as the President himself from the periphery took note of this momentous occasion.

With a smile as glazed as a doughnut, Dreyfus draped his arm around his star detective and did his best to take some of the credit that had slipped from his grasp and settled like a heavenly aura around Inspector Jacques Clouseau.

Many commented on how gracious the chief inspector had been.

Even his deputy Renard noted that Dreyfus had had tears in his eyes, one of which had begun to rather noticeably twitch.

FOURTEEN

Medal of Honor

On a glorious sunny morning, flags flapping in a gentle breeze, the President and the members of his Medal of Honor committee, as well as various other dignitaries and honored guests, assembled on a tri-colored-bunting-bedecked reviewing stand in the Presidential Gardens, gathered before an audience of press and public.

They were here to honor a great French—indeed, renowned international—detective.

Appropriately, the official band had struck up La Marseillaise.

On the stage, one of the committee members was among the nation's most celebrated crime-fighters—Chief Inspector Charles Dreyfus. It was not he who was being honored, however; actually, he had been selected to have the honor of *bestowing* the honors. Right now he stood somewhat uncomfortably beside Justice Minister Clochard, who bore a red velvet pillow on which were arrayed two ribboned medals.

Two other detectives stood onstage, in full formal gendarme uniform: Clouseau and Ponton.

At the microphone, the President himself presided. He nodded to Dreyfus that—the band having completed the national anthem—the presentation would begin. Dreyfus nodded and smiled, his left eye twitching just a little, both eyes rather noticeably bloodshot.

"For service to the Republic of France," the President said, his voice amplified and sonorous as it floated out across the crowd, seated on folding chairs on the greenest of green lawns, "we award the Star of Valor to Gendarme Detective Gilbert Ponton of the Fourth Arrondissement."

Ponton stepped forward.

Rather stiffly, Dreyfus removed the smaller of the two medals from the velvet cushion, and joined Ponton toward the front of the stage, placing the ribbon around the big man's neck and pulling him forward with the hug and kiss-on-either-cheek that was a part of the honor.

"For exceptional bravery," the President went on, "and outstanding service to the people of France, we award this year's Medal of Honor to a man whose name will forever be synonymous with this celebrated case—dubbed by the world the Pink Panther Detective . . . Inspector Jacques Clouseau."

With precise military bearing, Clouseau came forward, and by the time he had reached Ponton's side, the applause and the cheers had built into thunder.

Chief Inspector Dreyfus took the Medal of Honor from Clochard's velvet pillow and, moving in a somewhat robotic manner, managed to place the ribbon around Clouseau's neck. For a long moment Dreyfus studied the Medal of Honor against the dark blue of Clouseau's uniform.

Clouseau whispered, "The emotion, she is great, is she not, Chief Inspector?"

Dreyfus drew in a deep breath and subjected himself to the ceremonial hug and kisses, and retreated, giving the heroes of the morning their moment. Perhaps, one day, his would come, as well.

In the first row, a proud Nicole applauded and beamed, and Clouseau felt his heart swell—the schoolboy crush on Xania could not compare to the depth of warmth he felt for this simple girl, who he felt sure . . . with his guidance . . . could some day rise to his level of accomplishment and intellect.

And warmth swelled within him for his partner, as well—his friend, Ponton, beside him. What a team they had made. What a team they *would* make . . .

A lesser man would have taken the day off, but Clouseau was if nothing else devoted to his work. He and Ponton shared an office now, though Nicole remained assigned to Chief Inspector Dreyfus.

Since the arrest of the Gluant killer, and the solving of the Pink Panther theft, the chief inspector had been quiet, even withdrawn. Clouseau had proven Dreyfus wrong, and in public—not a pill this proud man could easily swallow. Clouseau feared his superior officer had fallen into depression. He knew the man had emotions swirling within him, and he hoped to make Dreyfus, like Ponton, a friend and a colleague.

So Clouseau decided always to keep the chief inspector informed, when a particularly important case reared its head. Perhaps, then, Clouseau might one day be able to place a ribbon around the neck of Dreyfus.

The first opportunity came that very afternoon.

Clouseau grabbed his trenchcoat, called for Ponton to join him, and stopped at the chief inspector's office. Nicole, at her desk in the reception area, did not announce Clouseau.

"Excuse me, Chief Inspector," Clouseau said, leaning in the office, "but I have just been notified that the Gas-Mask Bandits have made the escape in Italy this morning . . . and they have just been seen committing the crime in progress near the Pont de la Tournelle. I have summoned a car, and will keep you informed!"

Dreyfus was already on his feet and out from behind his new desk. "Thank you, Clouseau—but I'll take charge of this one, personally!"

"It would be my honor to assist you, Chief Inspector."

Soon the three men—Dreyfus working to keep up with Clouseau and Ponton—were racing down the imposing front stairs of the Palais de la Justice. A police van was waiting, and Ponton took the wheel, Clouseau the passenger's seat, while an eager Dreyfus climbed in back.

Through the streets of Paris the van raced, taking corners on two wheels, its siren screaming— the Gas-Mask Bandits might be back, but the greatest detectives in France were on the case!

Ponton pulled up at a curb, but it was too close to the wall for Clouseau to get out.

"Pull up!" he cried. "The time, she is wasting!"

Ponton did as he was told, but before Clouseau could climb out, Dreyfus was opening the back door and saying, "No, Clouseau, this time *I'm* in charge. This time the credit will be *mine* . . ."

And Dreyfus tumbled over the half-wall of the bridge they were parked on, his long drawn-out cry interrupted by a very big splash.

The two looked down sympathetically at the chief inspector floundering in the Seine, his eye twitching, his mouth open in a scream gone silent, a kind of madness building in his expression.

Leaning against the short wall beside his partner, Clouseau gave Ponton a look touched by pity, sighing, "A great detective, the chief inspector . . . but clumsy."

And while gendarmes below fished Dreyfus from the river, Inspector Clouseau and his partner returned to the chase.